PRAISE FOR

LUMBERJANES

UNICORN POWER!

★ "This middle-grade charmer can make even the coldest, bleakest day feel like a sunny day at summer camp."
—*Kirkus Reviews*

"A smart, silly, fast-paced adventure."
—*School Library Journal*

"Full of puns, adventure, magical creatures, and girl power aplenty." —*Booklist*

"Destined to delight." —*Shelf Awareness*

"Seamlessly mixes fantasy, adventure, and just plain fun!"
—*School Library Connection*

THE LUMBERJANES NOVELS

BOOK ONE: Unicorn Power!

BOOK TWO: The Moon Is Up

BOOK THREE: The Good Egg

BOOK FOUR: Ghost Cabin

LUMBERJANES

UNICORN POWER!

BOOK ONE

BY **MARIKO TAMAKI**

ILLUSTRATED BY **BROOKLYN ALLEN**

BASED ON THE LUMBERJANES COMICS
CREATED BY SHANNON WATTERS,
GRACE ELLIS, NOELLE STEVENSON & BROOKLYN ALLEN

AMULET BOOKS
NEW YORK

CATALOGING-IN-PUBLICATION DATA HAS BEEN APPLIED FOR AND MAY BE OBTAINED FROM THE LIBRARY OF CONGRESS.

PAPERBACK ISBN 978-1-4197-2726-9

BOOK DESIGN BY CHAD W. BECKERMAN

PUBLISHED IN PAPERBACK IN 2019 BY AMULET BOOKS, AN IMPRINT OF ABRAMS. ORIGINALLY PUBLISHED IN HARDCOVER BY AMULET BOOKS IN 2017.

PRINTED AND BOUND IN USA
10 9 8 7 6 5 4 3 2 1

ABRAMS The Art of Books
195 Broadway, New York, NY 10007
abramsbooks.com

FOR ALL THE
LUMBERJANES
OUT THERE.
AND FOR
HEATHER XO.
–M.T.

LUMBERJANES

FIELD MANUAL

LUMBERJANES PLEDGE

I solemnly swear to do my best
Every day, and in all that I do,
To be brave and strong,
To be truthful and compassionate,
To be interesting and interested,
To pay attention and question
The world around me,
To think of others first,
To always help and protect my friends

And to make the world a better place
For Lumberjane scouts
And for everyone else.

THEN THERE'S A LINE ABOUT GOD, OR WHATEVER

PART ONE

[illegible] in this matching contest. You need to [illegible] outdoor housekeeping, in all its forms, before [illegible] a real explorer or camper.

[illegible] out of doors is just outside your door, whether [illegible] are a city girl or a country dweller. Get acquainted with what is near at hand and then be ready to range farther afield. Discover how to use all the ways of getting to take over hill and dale, to satisfy that outdoor appetite with food cooked to a turn over a hunters' fire, to live comfortably in the open—all of these seem especially important to a Camp Fire Girl. She is a natural born traveler and pathfinder. She has an urge to get out and match her wits with the elements, to feel the wind, the sun, and even the rain against her face.

If you know how to lay and follow trails, how to walk without getting tired, how to build a fire that will burn, and how to protect yourself from the weather and other more important (or even supernatural) forces, your wits [illegible]

LIVING THE PLANT LIFE BADGE

"Herbivores eat shoots and lots o' leaves."

Among the many things that Lumberjanes love, the great outdoors is pretty tops on the list. Not surprising, as the great outdoors, so named because it is really, really great, is full of so many things for Lumberjanes to learn about and enjoy. Majestic forests, roaring streams, towering mountains—all make up the splendor of the natural world. But also included in the natural world are many smaller wonders: toadstools, caterpillars, lichen, and moss, to name just a few.

A Lumberjane must learn to appreciate and understand, and ultimately protect, all the parts of the natural world. Take, for example, the multitudes of plants that live and grow in the forest, plants that make oxygen, that feed the forest in numerous ways. The forest is rich with plants that, if you are paying close attention . . .

CHAPTER 1

It was a gorgeous day. In the woods just outside Miss Qiunzella Thiskwin Penniquiqul* Thistle Crumpet's Camp for Hardcore Lady-Types, the trees stood tall, reaching their branches up to the sky in a long, peaceful, never-ending stretch. The sun shone through the whispering leaves, scattering little pieces of light over the forest floor like a woodland disco.

It was a perfect day to be a Lumberjane, frankly, because every day, if you use it right, is a perfect day to be a Lumberjane. Because Lumberjanes are awesome: dedicated to friendship, learning, curiosity, and caring, to jumping into adventure with full hearts.

On this particular day, five Lumberjanes—the members of Roanoke cabin—wandered through the forest intent on making this day all kinds of wicked cool.

* Pronounced *Penny-quee-quellle*

There was April, the redhead skipping ahead with a look of determination and her ever-present notebook tucked under her arm. April was small but mighty, embodying a distinct April-like ferocity, a certain April-esque drive, as anyone who had ever arm-wrestled with her would know.

There was Jo, walking tall with long, steady strides. Jo always had a multi-tool tucked in her pocket and a serious look on her long face. Sometimes when Jo looked at the world, she saw all these little numbers and calculations in her head, little bits of how she knew the world worked.

There was Mal, who could play guitar and was also the best hide-and-seek and capture-the-flag player ever. Mal was a master strategist and also usually the first person to notice when something was weird. Also she hated bodies of water. Hated. Bodies. Of water.

As they walked through the woods, Mal held hands with Molly.

Molly was the only person in her cabin with her own personal raccoon hat, which was actually a raccoon named Bubbles. Molly had sunny blonde hair she kept in a braid, and a gentle voice. Molly was pretty good at spotting the best in the people around her, although sometimes she had trouble doing that for herself.

Bouncing somewhere around the back of the group was Ripley, the blue streak in her hair swinging in front of her eyes. Ripley, incidentally, gave the best hugs, and when she liked things, liked them A LOT.

"Right!" April flipped her notebook open to her checklist. "So far, we've got three types of moss . . ."

"Cushion, haircap, and mood." Jo ticked them off on her fingers.

"Hairy mood cushion moss!" Ripley chuckled, bouncing between trees. "Moody hair cushion moss!"

"Three types of vines," April continued.

"Trumpet, honeysuckle, and *Clematis tangutica*," Jo added, carefully enunciating TAN-GUT-TIC-AHHHH.

April tapped her pencil on her notepad. "Perfect! We just need one more flowering plant and . . . we've got our LIVING THE PLANT LIFE badges!"

The Living the Plant Life badge was the ultimate all-encompassing super-nerdy greenery-loving badge. It was going to look great on April's already crowded badge sash, which contained badges for lovers of sailing, hiking, running, and punning. As well as many other things. Maybe she would even need to get another sash. THE DREAM! DOUBLE SASH!

April sighed contentedly. Everything was going according to plan.

"There's more sun in the clearing up ahead," Jo said, pointing. "Maybe we'll find something flower-like there."

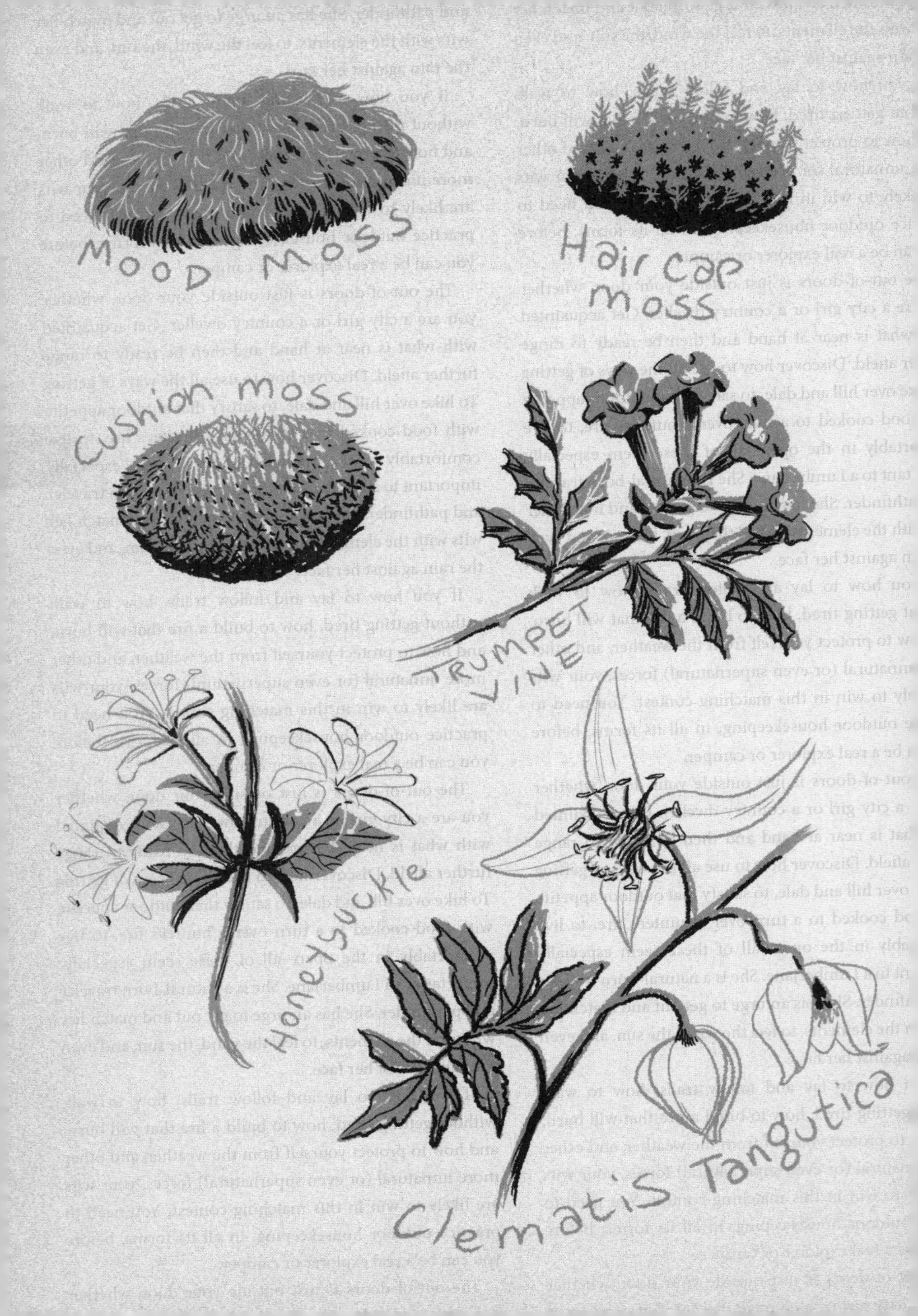
Mood Moss
Hair cap Moss
Cushion moss
TRUMPET VINE
Honeysuckle
Clematis Tangutica

"YIPPEE!" Ripley cartwheeled ahead and the rest of the scouts followed.

"I love that one of the flowers was called a beardtongue," Molly said. "Whoever gets to name plants has the best job ever."

"I think if it's called a beardtongue, it should LOOK like a tongue," Mal noted. "Or a beard." Beardtongue looked more like red trumpets than beards.

"Maybe it's a metaphor," Molly offered.

"A metaphor for what?" Mal laughed.

The girls came to a stop in the clearing.

Ripley hopped over to a giant tree covered in bumpy fungus. "YO! These mushrooms look like noses," she said, peering at the rubbery fungi dotting the tree trunk.

Molly turned and noticed a small green plant curled up next to Mal's toe. "Watch out! Poison ivy!"

"WHAT?" Mal shot up like she'd been electrocuted. She shook her foot violently.

"Hey," April said, looking up from the spot where she'd been poking around for flowers, "if it was Valentine's Day, we'd be looking for a willyoube vine! Right? Get it?"

Another thing about April: Few people liked puns as much as she did.

Mal continued to take a series of tiny steps away from the potential poison ivy, keeping a watchful eye on the bright green menace. You know, just in case it made a move.

Jo was bent forward, in deep tractor-beam-level concentration as she peered through the lens of her new invention, the Micro-Focus Lens. The pink and green leaves of the plant on the other side of the lens twisted into view. People who look at things as closely as Jo did often know that they're rarely only what they appear to be at first glance. In this case, what looked like a shiny, smooth leaf to the naked eye was spiky under the lens, a sea of interlocked scales with sharp pointed edges like a lizard's back.

Jo squinted and pressed her lips together in determination as she twisted the dial next to the lens to try and get a better view. The leaf clicked into a higher resolution, but then went fuzzy again. Something was affecting the magnification. Jo sighed. Invention requires trial and error, which means when you invent something, the only way to know if it works is to test it. Sometimes this process takes a very long time.

Jo knew this, in part, because one of Jo's dads (she had two) invented a rocket. It took him 1,034 tries. That's a lot of tries. All the rockets were named Diana after Diana Ross, because her dad said Diana Ross had a unique star quality.

Jo wondered if the workshop back at camp, where she could frequently be found rummaging for parts or throwing up sparks with the welding equipment, had the parts she needed. Momentarily, she wished she had access to the extravagant lab her dads had set up for her at home.

Maybe she could take apart her fancy phone and use some of the circuitry from that . . .

A few feet away from Jo, April nibbled on the pencil gripped between her teeth, her brow furrowed in resolve as she scanned the forest floor for a speck of something other than green.

Green.

Green.

Green.

Blue?

BLUE!

Nestled in among a patch of fluffy ferns was a tiny blue flower with diamond-shaped petals.

Reaching into her back pocket, April pulled out her *Lumberjanes Flora and Fauna Guide*. The book was old and squished, probably because it had been crushed into so many pockets over the years. The spine was cracked and taped and taped again. The corners were worn and stained with streaks of grass green.

April thumbed through the pages. "Chrysanthemum? Crocus?"

She flipped the page and a small square of paper came loose and fluttered into her hand. It was a faded sketch of a blue flower with . . . hey! . . . diamond-shaped petals! Under the drawing someone had written, in delicate cursive, "Clow Bell."

On the edge of the paper, in the same delicate text: "Previously sited and not recorded, but here noted as new, a very curious plant. Edible? Maybe. Credible? Yes. Celestial? . . ."

"Hey, guys!" April called out, waving the picture. "GUYS! CLOWBELL!" she cried, triumphant.

At the exact same time, Ripley, shooting up into the air and pointing over April's shoulder, screamed probably one of the top ten words a person can possibly scream.

UNICORN POWER!

CHAPTER 2

What Ripley actually said would probably be better translated as "UUUUUUNNNNNIIIIICOOOORRRRRNNNNNN!!!!!"

Because from the instant the first vowel left her lips, Ripley was already zooming after the unicorn as it darted off with a flick of its sparkly purple tail.

When she was really, really excited, Ripley could hit the speed of a thousand Ripleys, which is very, very fast.

At this moment, Ripley was very very very excited. And so very very very fast.

Of course, wouldn't you run superfast if you'd loved unicorns your whole life and even had your OWN (stuffed) unicorn called Mr. Sparkles and then you saw AN ACTUAL unicorn running through the forest?

I think so.

The rest of Roanoke cabin took a(nother) moment to assess the situation.

"Ah," Jo said.

"Ah!" Molly agreed.

"Unicorn!" Mal gasped.

"Ripley!" April cried.

RIPLEY!

With that settled, the rest of the Lumberjanes were in hot pursuit.

The number one rule of being a Lumberjane: Lumberjanes stick together!

CHAPTER 3

Of the many things there are to know about unicorns, which is a lot, one relatively vital fact is that unicorns, when they're moving on the ground, enjoy taking a serpentine, or twisty-turny, route.

No unicorn has been able to explain why this is; it's just something they do.

April, who took the lead in the unicorn-and-Ripley pursuit, had spent some time as a kid reading books about unicorn adventures. Some of her favorites included *Harvey the Amazing Unicorn and His Unicorn Friends*, *Unicorns on Ice*, *Just Enough Unicorns*, and the less popular but still riveting *Unicorns Go to the Beach*.

(April's notebook contained several pages of detailed notes on various creatures the members of Roanoke cabin had encountered so far during their amazing adventures. The unicorn section was a little thin, though, as this was Roanoke's first unicorn sighting!

How exciting is that!?)

April's readings did not actually say anything about how to chase a unicorn, but April was a quick study.

"ZIGZAG," she hollered back to the other Lumberjanes, raising one arm and jerking it back and forth. "It's running in a ZIG! ZAG!"

Jo glanced down and noticed that the unicorn wasn't leaving any hoofprints on the ground. Not even in the dainty layer of cushion moss that covered the rocks they stepped on to cross the creek.

"Interesting," Jo said.

The raccoon, Bubbles, who had been sleeping peacefully on Molly's head, was now very awake. The breeze rippled through his fur as he clung for dear life to the top of Molly's head while she raced after Jo who was chasing after April who was in hot pursuit of Ripley who was tailing a unicorn. Bubbles chirped a curious chirp, like, "Where are we going and why are we going so fast?"

As Mal sprinted through the trees behind the others, she looked up at the sky. She wondered exactly where it was they were going, while noticing that the trees of the new forest they were running through were thicker and puffier, like green storm clouds. The thought slipped into her head, like a thread through a needle, that Jen, their camp counselor, who was prone to worrying about them, might be wondering where they were right about now.

"Hey," she hollered, "should we b—" Mal looked forward again and noticed everyone had stopped running. "YEAGH!"

YEAGH isn't a word, but a sound that basically translates to, "Wow, I wish I had known we were stopping."

It is very hard to go from traveling at superfast breakneck speed to a dead halt. Which is why Mal crashed into Molly crashed into Jo crashed into April.

"OOF!"

"OOOF!"

"OOOOF!"

"WHAAAH!"

By the last WHAAAH, they had all stopped. If by "stopped" we mean "crashed into each other."

"Our mass-sprinting technique needs immediate and drastic improvement," April groaned, crawling out from the bottom of the pile of Lumberjanes.

"We need to come up with a stopping technique," Jo added, brushing pine needles off her hoodie.

"Yes," Molly sighed, brushing off Bubbles, who was now thoroughly coated in forest floor. "Let's do that soon."

Next to the heap of Roanoke cabin, Ripley, who had narrowly missed the big Roanoke pileup, was dancing a jig, her hand clasped over her mouth.

"Look! Look! Look!" she squealed gleefully through her fingertips. "The unicorn! He's munching!"

"AWWWWW!" cooed the Lumberjanes in chorus, starry eyed.

"Now that," April said, "is positively adorable."

Because AW! Come on! What could be cuter than a unicorn standing, placid, which is to say, calm, in a small clearing in the trees, daintily snacking on what April now knew to be a Clow Bell?

Very little comes to mind.

From a few feet away, the Lumberjanes could see that the unicorn's tail and mane weren't just purple but a mix of every purple-like color (violet, maroon, lavender, and indigo), combined with spun gold. The rest of his coat was a soft, pearlescent shade of gray, with spots of white on his hindquarters. His horn was silver.

April straightened the white bow that was keeping her red curls, now full of leaves, off her face. "Okay, so we have a unicorn and a Ripley. So now we just need to . . ." April paused and twitched her button nose.

"Huh." Jo sniffed the air, the hood of her hoodie still full of pine needles.

"Ummm," Mal noted, making sure all her earrings and nose rings were still in place, "do you guys smell that?"

The rest of the cabin lifted their noses to the wind, which was blowing in from the unicorn's direction. All five girls simultaneously clamped their hands over their noses.

"WHOA!" They all agreed in unison. Because. WHOA.

"Is that smell . . . UNICORN?" April said in the nasal tone necessary when you are speaking with your hand on your nose.

"That is bad," Molly said.

"It's flagrantly noxious," April said.

Mal agreed. "It's bad with sprinkles on top."

REALLY. REALLY. REALLY BAD.

"So. Unicorns smell like armpits and anchovies," Jo said. "That's unexpected."

"But then again," Molly added, with a smile mostly covered by her hand, "it seems kind of expectedly unexpected."

Mal grinned. Because Molly was right—the unexpected happens all the time when you're a Lumberjane.

April pulled out her notebook and flipped through her notes. "And undocumented," she added, making a note so it WOULD be.

Ripley, taking the smallest, tiptoe steps, moved toward the unicorn. "Hey there," she said, in a bedtime-story type of voice, "my name is Ripley and I promise I won't do anything to hurt you ever, ever, ever."

The unicorn looked up from munching and appeared to take in his surroundings. He looked left and right and then at Ripley, who continued her careful steps. He let out a small, twinkly neigh.

Ripley stepped up to the unicorn, hands held out, palms up, as a sign that she was a safe creature. The unicorn touched his velvety nose to Ripley's outstretched hand. Ripley's heart felt like it was going to burst with a great big PLURT!

"Contact," April whispered to Jo with a grin.

Ripley, her hand pressed against the unicorn's neck, turned back to the rest of the cabin, her face twisted into a worried frown. "Hey," she said, "I think he's LOST."

April looked at the unicorn, which looked back at April with an expression that was difficult to decipher, because unicorns, like buffalo, ferrets, and horses (not surprisingly), can be hard to read. Still, April put her hands on her hips. She knew exactly what to do next.

"Lumberjanes to the rescue!"

CHAPTER 4

There is a long and complex history of people finding magical creatures like unicorns and taking them home.

This is, generally, a terrible idea.

Unicorns, like most magical creatures, are not pets.

The only thing that's a pet is a pet.

The exception is magical kittens, which are magical but also pets, but also a huge handful to care for.

You think you know how to handle magical animals, you think, "Hey, no problem." But that is rarely true.

Magical creatures take up a lot of space, they are very picky eaters, and sometimes they breathe fire or blow long, sharp projectiles of ice out their nostrils.

A Lumberjane respects all creatures of the wild, in all their shapes and sizes. Lumberjanes know that fauna (creatures) are often best off where you find them, whether that's in the forest, at the bottom of a lake, or in a swamp.

(Unless one day you meet a raccoon and he seems lonely and likes sleeping on your head like a hat, that's a completely different thing, obviously.)

Ripley didn't want to take the unicorn home with her, tempting though it was. But she did want to help him get unlost.

The unicorn now looked very vexed, turned his head this way and that, and whinnied worriedly.

"We need a plan," April said. "Toadstool formation!"

Toadstool formation is distinct in that you stand in a triangle instead of a circle. For whatever reason, it works really well for coming up with ideas.

Jo snapped her fingers. "Hey! If all unicorns smell like this one," she noted, "then maybe we could smell the herd."

April pointed at Jo. "Yes! I like this. This sounds like the start of a good plan."

Mal leaned over to Molly and whispered, "Hey, is it me or is smelling a herd kind of hilarious?"

"Agreed," Molly whispered back.

"How do we find a smell?" Ripley asked, gazing over at the still-nervous-looking unicorn and thinking that he smelled like a very old cheese sandwich she found in the back of her mom's minivan once. But that was okay because the unicorn was also very, very soft.

April raised her hand, because that's what you do in class when you have an idea and some habits are hard to break. "Oh, oh, I know! If unicorns eat Clow Bells," she said, "then we should look where the Clow Bells grow! Which is—"

"What's a cow bell?" Molly asked.

"A CLOW Bell. I just found it in the flora and fauna guide!" April grabbed the book out of her pocket again. "Actually, it was kind of a mysterious drawing stuck into the guide, but still . . ."

April flipped to the map at the back of the book, which was covered in little symbols showing what plants could be found in different regions. Someone had drawn a bunch of little diamonds for the Clow Bells, dotted all over the map. "Looks like there's a lot of Clow Bells growing . . . a little north of here!" she told the group. With her free hand, April pulled her compass out of her pocket and waited for the needle to point north.

"And if we start walking, we'll know we're headed in the right direction when we smell something that smells like the back seat of a really old school bus!" Molly cheered.

April's eyes sparkled with April-like determination. "Time to stop horsin' around and get movin'!" she said.

"Is a unicorn a horse?" Molly wondered.

The Lumberjanes turned and looked at the unicorn, who looked back at them not so much expectantly but inquisitively.

CHAPTER 5

It is an incredibly handy thing to know how to move various large objects. There are several different Lumberjane badges that cover this skill, many of which April had already acquired.

When it comes to moving unicorns, most people just wing it. This is probably the best approach, given that how you get a unicorn to move largely depends on the specific unicorn. Unicorns are a lot like people: Some of them are easily moved; some of them would rather just stay put and see what's on TV.

Very quickly it became clear that this particular unicorn, while lost, was not sure he wanted to go where the members of Roanoke cabin—April specifically—had planned.

At first, the Lumberjanes thought they would just start walking and the unicorn would follow.

That didn't happen.

The Lumberjanes took a few steps forward into the forest but then realized they were without the magical creature.

"UGH. He's not budging." April squinted at the unicorn, trying to read his unicorn brain. "Maybe a zigzag would be more constructive."

April, Jo, and Mal walked back to the unicorn and then started north again, zigzagging at a slow jog. Nothing. They trudged back through the woods to find the unicorn standing there, looking at them, possibly quizzically.

Although, as we said, it's hard to tell.

Who knew unicorns were stubborn? In all the books April had read, the unicorns were mostly . . . noble.

Mal and Molly tried calling the unicorn. "HERE, UNICORN," they trilled as they walked backward, waving their hands to get his attention.

That also didn't work.

Ripley had the idea to push the unicorn from behind. Which they all quickly admitted was a horrible idea. Unicorns, on all four hoofs, are as immovable as a house.

Maybe more.

Technically, Jo knew, to move a house you needed a unified hydraulic jacking system. Not that you would use that to move a unicorn. Unless . . .

"Well," Molly said, taking a break from unicorn shoving to catch her breath, "maybe he's not lost. Maybe this is just where he wants to be."

Ripley shook her head. "He's lost. I know it." Putting both her hands on the unicorn's cheeks, Ripley pressed her forehead against his broad, but difficult to interpret, white face. "I can feel it."

The unicorn blinked his blue eyes and snorted.

"Maybe we just need to sing him a unicorn song," Ripley suggested. "You know, it could be like . . ." Ripley tilted her head and, holding her palms up to the sky, started to sing in a sweet, high-pitched little voice. "La la la unicorn soooong! La la la la uuuuuuunicorn song."

When that didn't work, she started . . . kind of . . . yelling the song. "LA LA LA UNICORN SOOOONG! LA! LA! LA! UUUUNICORN SSSSOOOONGGGG!!!!"

Nope.

"Hey." Molly reached down and grabbed a small bouquet of what Clow Bells were left. "What if we lure him with these?"

Molly took a few steps in the direction April said they needed to go, turned, and shook the Clow Bells at the unicorn. "Hey! Unicorn! Uh. You hungry?" She called out.

The unicorn lifted his head.

"Come on," Ripley whispered encouragingly, putting her hand on the unicorn's neck and taking a small step forward. "You can do it."

The unicorn swished his tail, whinnied, and moved toward Molly.

April pulled the last Clow Bell she could find out of the ground in case they lost momentum.

Aaaand they were off! The Lumberjanes, and the unicorn, started walking northish, still in a zigzag pattern but at a regular speed. Everyone was feeling a combination of elated (that the unicorn was now moving), enchanted (to be walking so close to an enchanted creature), and a little overwhelmed by the olfactory experience (the smell).

"I hope we find his family, herd, whatever," Mal said to Molly, as the two of them walked a bit ahead, and a bit upwind, of the unicorn. Mal wondered if the unicorn was worried he wouldn't see his other unicorns ever again.

Molly was thinking about what it was like to feel like a unicorn. Molly sometimes felt like a unicorn when she was with her family.

Jo spotted the herd first, although everybody smelled something before they hit the edge of the forest, where the trees gave way to a lush meadow of green. "Ursula K. Le Guin! We found it!"

In and among the green, there was a sea, a rainbow, of

unicorns, all with different-colored tails (reds and blues and yellows and greens). Their horns twinkled in the sun as they munched and meandered in lazy zigzags.

"Wow," Molly breathed, in awe. "It's like a coloring book come to life."

"To the max," Jo added.

"It's positively Yayoi Kusama," April sighed.

The previously lost, now found unicorn gave a little neigh and trotted forward, away from the Lumberjanes, through the grass, waving his tail.

The other unicorns stopped munching and raised their heads. A few of them neighed back at the unicorn as if to say, "Hey, where have you been?"

"Yay!" Ripley cheered, twirling. "Unicorn is home! YAY UNICORN!"

"Wow, there's . . . uh . . . Clow Bells everywhere!" Jo noted, taking in the sight of rainbow unicorns and Clow Bells as far as the eye could see.

"YAY CLOW BELLS!" Ripley cheered again, jumping up and down in the tall grass. "It's their home," she sang. "YAY Clow Bell Unicorn City!"

Molly and Mal simultaneously had a thought that Clow Bell Unicorn City would be a really great band name.

Ripley was so happy she started doing a happy dance. Ripley had amazing happy dances. They were springy and slippy and involved a lot of Ripley being up in the air and not necessarily on the ground. She waved her arms in the air and hopped from one foot to the other. Ripley's dad said she was born dancing. That was probably true.

Mal and Molly smiled as Ripley did her dance.

Jo smiled too. "Hey, we did it! Not bad for a day's scouting."

"Agreed," April said. Then, looking up, she spotted a thing that was pretty easy to spot because it was gigantic.

CHAPTER 6

"Humongous," April said, because *humongous* was a much better word.

Jo raised an eyebrow. "Holy Junko Tabei! That is pretty cool."

What they were looking at, past the fields of green and blue Clow Bells, past the unicorns with their rainbow tails, past all these things and stretching up to the sky, was a mountain. And not even just any mountain, a mountain that seemed to be as big as the sky. A mountain made of rock that changed from purple to blue to gray to purple again as the sun grazed over its face. A mountain covered in bits of sparkly whiteness outlining jagged peaks.

April tipped her head back. "Wow, you can't even see the top, even if I tip my head back as far as it will go."

The very tip-top of the mountain, or at least as far up as April could see, was ringed with peachy pink clouds. Like a halo.

Jo looked up. "It's pretty awesome," she concurred. "What do you think it's called?"

"I don't know," April said. "But we sh—"

"MALMOLLYJORIPLEYAPRIL!"

Mal, Molly, Jo, Ripley, and April spun around. Emerging from the forest was Jen, general smart person, amazing astronomer, Roanoke camp counselor extraordinaire.

Jen did not look amused. She looked very very unamused. Her Lumberjanes uniform, which she usually wore in this way that looked super profesh, was so soaking wet it wasn't even its regular green and yellow. Her superlong black hair was waterlogged and hung down on her shoulders like seaweed. Her little green beret, which usually looked pretty jaunty, sat on the top of her head like a soggy paper plate. Jen stomped through the grass toward the scouts. Her shoes made squitch, squitch, squitch sounds. She looked like someone who had spent a very long time looking for a group of scouts who should have been in a place and weren't in that place.

The members of Roanoke cabin were rarely where they were supposed to be. Mostly because there were so many other places to be!

"JEN!" They all cried in unison.

"Hey, Jen," Jo added. "Are you okay? What happened to you?"

"Hey, Jen," Molly wondered. "Did you fall in a lake or something?"

Mal had the distinct sense that "what happened to you" was not the main question to be answered right now.

"Funny you should ask—YES, I DID! How did that happen, Jen? Let me tell you! I LEFT YOU FOR TEN MINUTES," Jen raved, waving her arms in the air like someone trying to catch a cab in the rain. "TEN MINUTES! And all you had to do was take a teeny-tiny part of your day to look for FLOWERS. FLOWERS! But no! I come back and you've all just POOF!"

"Actually," Molly considered, "it was more like ZIP!"

"We were looking for flowers!" April explained. "And we found Clow Bells, and then we saw—"

Jen shook her head, sending out a shower of water droplets. "JUST ONCE, ONCE, I'd like to tell you guys to do something and have you do it."

Jen pinched the bridge of her nose and took a deep breath. "Find your calm center, Jen," she whispered. "It's in there somewhere."

Jen was an amazing camp counselor, if sometimes very stressed because she was constantly dealing with campers who refused to follow the very-clear-and-for-their-own-safety rules. Rules that Jen liked because they were the glue that held things together. Rules were a Band-Aid, a safeguard, and a necessity—and, HECK, rules were RULES!

Rules, like always tell your counselor where you're going, and don't run off to catch a unicorn without telling your camp counselor first, were IMPORTANT.

Jen stopped, possibly taking in, for the first time, the fact that the members of Roanoke cabin weren't alone. "Is that a field of unicorns behind you?"

The unicorns stopped munching momentarily and looked at Jen. One of them whinnied as if to say, "Yes. Yes it is."

"Yup," Jo concurred.

"We found the Clow Bells," April continued in rapid fire, "which, it turns out, unicorns eat! Which I should probably document—"

Jen's eyes widened. "Well, that's . . ."

"Also—" April began.

But then Jen clamped her hand over her nose. "What is that smell?!"

"The unicorns," Molly finished. "Sort of . . . smell. Bad."

"They ACTUALLY smell bad," Mal clarified.

"AREN'T THEY AWESOME!?" Ripley cheered.

"They smell like sweat sock stew," Jen said, her eyes watering.

"Ripley saw the unicorn and we chased him," April started up again, because there was so much more to say, "and . . . this is a long story but . . . then when we found the unicorn, he was lost so—"

"All right," Jen sighed. Then she put one hand on her hip and kept the other on her nose. "If you guys want dinner, we need to get back to camp, PRONTO!"

Mal and Molly and Jo weren't sure if they still wanted dinner, now that they were thinking about sock stew, but it seemed like a good idea to head back.

Ripley took one last moment to say good-bye to her unicorn, who seemed happy to be back chomping Clow Bells with his fellow unicorns. Ripley gave the unicorn a hug and the unicorn took a moment to nudge Ripley's back with his nose. Which is sort of a unicorn hug.

"I'm going to call you Dr. Twinkle," Ripley whispered into the supersoft unicorn fur.

Dr. Twinkle whinnied as if to say, "Okay, whatever you want, kid. I'm going to go back to my munching if you don't mind."

April stood in the field. The unicorns grazed and flicked their rainbow tails, and behind them, the impossibly (except nothing is impossible) colossal mountain stretched up almost past the sky. It was a kind of perfect Lumberjane moment. It was—

"APRIL!" Jen hollered, tromping back toward camp. "LET'S GO!"

"Smell you later," April whispered. Then she turned on her heels and headed back to camp. "COMING!"

CHAPTER 7

Located in the heart of the forest, at the entrance to the Lumberjanes camp, is a tall wooden archway with a sign that reads, MISS QIUNZELLA THISKWIN PENNIQUIQUL THISTLE CRUMPET'S CAMP FOR HARDCORE LADY-TYPES.

If you look closely, you will see that the Hardcore Lady-Types part of the sign is actually another piece of wood nailed onto the original sign. Underneath, the original sign might have read CAMP FOR GIRLS OF CHIPMUNKS OF PONIES OF GIRLISH CHIPMUNKPONIES. But clearly someone, at some time, decided to make it clear that Hardcore Lady-Types were top on the agenda at Miss Qiunzella Thiskwin Penniquiqul Thistle Crumpet's Camp.

Hanging under the archway is another sign that reads, FRIENDSHIP TO THE MAX, because being a friend, a really amazing friend, is a big part of being a Lumberjane.

Miss Qiunzella Thiskwin Penniquiqul Thistle Crumpet's Camp has existed for more decades than anyone currently at the camp, or even on the board of directors, can say for sure. It is a camp for discoverers and adventurers, creative types and athletic types, and anyone who doesn't think they are or have a type.

Miss Qiunzella Thiskwin Penniquiqul Thistle Crumpet herself once proclaimed that a Lumberjane was anyone who had the gumption, the know-how, and the wherewithal to want to be something more than she was already. Miss Qiunzella herself was an inventor (credited with early designs of what would eventually become the elevator and Frisbee), a hot-air balloonist, an ardent cyclist (who once circled the globe on a bicycle), a sculptor, a fencing champion, and an overall hearty adventurer, who also pioneered early scuba gear. She was also the author of several short stories about Merfolk, collected in the books *A Lady's Under-the-Sea Summer Vacations with the Merfolk* and *Underwater Etiquette*.

Past the archway is a circle of cabins and a big open field, at the center of which is a flagpole flying the Lumberjanes' double-ax flag. The field also has tennis nets, a volleyball net, a stage, and a bunch of picnic benches for crafting or eating or hanging out. There's the beaver fire pit, guarded by several stoic beaver (and other animal) carvings, where marshmallows are roasted, ghost stories traded, and several folk songs have been written and sung. Just past the fire pit is the path that snakes up to the camp workshop, garage, and kiln, then the arts and crafts cabin, and down the path a bit, the camp library.

Generally, in the center of camp, in the big clearing next to the fire pit, there are tons and tons of scouts, doing what scouts do.

Which, on any given day, could be one of many many many things, including learning how to build a fire, a canoe, a cabin, or a kite; decorating a cake or a kimono; making brisket, cinnamon buns, or bagels. This is, of course, an abbreviated list, 'cause the actual complete list is really long.

Really really really long.

While the members of Roanoke cabin were finishing their Living the Plant Life badges and chasing unicorns that day, for example, the other Lumberjane scouts were doing yoga, shingling the roof of Zodiac cabin, learning cross-stitch embroidery, practicing cartography (which is mapmaking), and working on their Guerilla Girl, the latest dance craze going around camp. The Guerilla Girl is not a complicated dance. To do it right, you have to have a really good growl, know how to do the Yoko Ono Slide, and have a general knowledge of the history of women in art.

At that moment, though, it was time for dinner at the mess hall, so the clearing was mostly empty, except for Barney, who had completely forgotten all about dinner, which is something Barney, a member of Zodiac cabin, sometimes did when absorbed in stacks of books.

"Hey, Barney!" Jo, Ripley, Mal, and Molly waved as they headed to the mess hall.

"Hey," Barney waved back, a bit distracted.

Jen detoured to the cabin to change into a dry uniform. "Please, just this ONCE, go where you're supposed to go: DINNER."

Fully intending to EVENTUALLY go to dinner, April wandered over to Barney's picnic bench, just as Barney was pulling the fifth book of the evening off the tallest of the stacks.

Barney was a recent addition to the Lumberjane camp. When Roanoke first met Barney, they (Barney used they/them and not he/him) were a Scouting Lad. But being a Lumberjane was a WAY better fit, because Barney didn't feel like they were a lad. Barney was supersmart, with a thick swish of black hair that stuck straight up and out like the brim of a baseball cap. April thought Barney was a dapper dresser, which is not an easy thing to be when you wear a khaki Lumberjanes uniform every day. Actually, Barney was one of the only scouts who wore their uniform every day, because they liked the crispness of the uniform shirt, and the buttons and the kerchief.

"Hey!" April scootched in next to Barney on the bench. "How's Lumberjane life STACKING up these days?"

Barney gestured to their book spread. "Ha ha. Um. Pretty good! I'm trying to figure out what my next badge is going to be."

"You must have SO MANY Scouting Lad badges!" April knew Barney was supergood at making all different kinds of things and fixing things, and once they made an igloo, which is a house made of SNOW! "I mean you're so . . . multitalented!"

Barney flushed, embarrassed. "Um, thanks. I guess. Lumberjane scouts have so many wonderful badges to choose from, I want to catch up. I just need to pick—"

"Oh my gosh!" April threw her arms open. "There are SO MANY Lumberjane badges! Like there's If You Got It, Haunt It badge, that's a spooky one; there's The Mystery of History badge, that's a great one too, because if you don't learn history you're sure as shootin' going to repeat it."

Barney nodded. "Truth."

April tried to think of all the badges Barney could do. There really were a lot. "Also there's the Absence Makes the Heart Grow Fondant badge, that's for cake decorating, obviously." April's tone clearly indicated this was not her favorite badge. April's own attempt to get her Fondant badge had turned her off cake for a whole week.

Making roses out of fondant . . . really not as easy as it looks.

Barney sat up. "Cake decorating?"

"Oh uh, yeah." April turned to Barney's stacks of books. On top of one was a book about sailboats. Its leather binding smelled faintly of seawater and kelp. April snapped her fingers. "SAILING! You should totally get your Seas for the Day badge! That's with Seafarin' Karen! Seafarin' Karen is the best! Oh my gosh, you'll love it, it's so great. You can get your sailing badge and your Knot on Your Life badge and your For the Halibut badge, and you'll have THREE BADGES!"

"Hmmmm," Barney said, looking through their stack for another book they'd taken out of the library, *Pastry: A Confection*.

April was pretty jazzed at the idea of Barney learning how to sail. "Okay!" she chirped. She wrapped her arms around Barney and gave them a big squeeze. "I gotta go eat. I'm so glad you're a Lumberjane."

"Me too." Barney hugged back. Because it is awesome to be in a place where you feel like you can be you. "Hey! What's that smell?"

"Oh." April put her sleeve to her nose and gave it a sniff. "It's probably just a bit of leftover eau de unicorn. Unicorns smell like three-week-old chip dip. It's okay, I have three other sweaters just like this. Bye!"

And with that, April ran off to the mess hall, where chili night was already in full swing.

CHAPTER 8

The Lumberjanes Mess Hall was a big log cabin with long tables and benches that stretched the length of the room. At the front was a massive set of antlers and the Lumberjane crossed axes. On the west wall hung the banners of all the cabins. The east wall of the mess hall was covered in plaques commemorating Lumberjanes dining milestones, which were always evolving.

Current lauded achievements included:

Most Broccoli Eaten in One Sitting: Devineau Porcupine
Least Broccoli Eaten in One Sitting: Bichoo Porcupine
Biggest Pie Baked: Jenny Barry
Biggest Pie Eaten: Jenny Barry

Most Questions about Food Ingredients in One Meal: Marcey Max

Longest Continuous Spaghetti Slurp: Florence McÑally

Ripley was up there a few times for pancake achievements, including Most Pancakes in One Sitting (14 ¾).

Also the recipients of the Absence Makes the Heart Grow Fondant cake-decorating badge, the Kebab's Your Uncle badge, and the Gourmet It Over With badge had photographs of their great feats tacked to the wall. Which included a picture of Marvis McGonnall's four-tiered chocolate chocolate chip cake

shaped like a fire-breathing dragon—which breathed actual fire, and so was never actually eaten.

Rosie, camp director at Miss Qiunzella Thiskwin Penniquiqul Thistle Crumpet's Camp for Hardcore Lady-Types,

sat at the back of the hall, at the table closest to the kitchen next to her pair of titanium pepper-handling gloves. Rosie was as tall as a tree and wore big, thick, horn-rimmed glasses and, almost always, some form of plaid. She had a pile of red hair, secured with a red polka-dot handkerchief, which in addition to being stylish is just a handy thing to have around. Rosie liked to keep her sleeves rolled up and was the most hardcore person most people had ever met. She liked a good-quality belt to hitch things onto and boots that were good for getting around. She had an anchor tattooed on her neck, which April heard had been tattooed with real silver squid ink.

As the scouts braved their chili, Rosie whistled and whittled at her table, carving what looked like a bird beak out of a giant stump of wood with the blade of her ax.

By the time April burst into the mess hall, Jo, Mal, Molly, and Ripley were already seated in front of steaming bowls of Rosie's signature Vegan Inferno Six-Bean Chili, made from a secret recipe (which curiously involved seven beans) chock-full of spices so spicy at least two of them could actually blow your eyeballs out if mishandled.

"Hey!" April sang, plopping down in her seat at the Roanoke table. "Is it just me or is it a little CHILI in here?"

"Careful," Jo warned, "it's crazy spicy today. I think Rosie might have harvested some new peppers from her garden." She plucked a ruby-red pepper from her spoon and held it up. "Some sort of new species," she mused.

Molly pulled her long blonde hair up and tucked it under her raccoon. Two spoons in and her neck and cheeks were flushed cherry red. Molly's parents didn't put anything but salt and pepper on their food. Sometimes not even pepper.

Molly's mom said pepper was "flashy."

Mal gulped from her glass of soy milk. "What the Ella Fitzgerald?!" she gasped. "I think my teeth are melting."

The noise of the mess hall, as usual, was deafening. It was the sounds of a camp full of hardcore lady types talking about what they did that day and what they were going to do tomorrow, which can get pretty loud.

Walcott cabin were busy plotting their strategy for the next dodgeball tournament, which Walcott pretty much always dominated.

Roswell cabin, infamously obsessed with really hot food, were having a contest to see who could eat the most raw chilies dipped in chili.

April took a teeny-tiny bite of chili, really just the edge of a bean. A thick wave of what felt like actual fire flooded her face, neck, and, curiously, feet. A single tear dripped down her cheek. "Good," she managed hoarsely. "A little spicy."

"Good evening, scouts."

The girls all looked up. Rosie stood next to their table with a handful of Living the Plant Life badges, which she lobbed onto the table. "Congratulations. It's not an easy badge to get."

Jo, whose tongue was fully singed, nodded.

"Thanks," Mal managed through the smoke collecting in her mouth.

Rosie leaned on the handle of her ax. "I came to my love of the botanical world late in life, but it is crucial Lumberjane know-how. A plant could save your tail."

April nodded, her brain flooded with images of flying heroic plants.

"Because of the medicinal qualities," Molly guessed.

"Sure. That too." Rosie slipped off her glasses and gave them a polish on her shirt. "The key thing to remember is, a Lumberjane is always prepared, and part of preparation is knowledge. Knowledge—of flora, fauna, basic mechanics—can be all that stands between you and a night on a frozen lake with a half-eaten canoe."

April's eyes popped open. HALF-EATEN CANOE? WHAT EATS A CANOE?

Fortunately, Mal missed that moment because the flames that seemed to be shooting out of her ears distracted her. Mal probably wouldn't have wanted to think too much about the possibility of having her canoe eaten on the edge of a frozen lake. Because lake.

Rosie slipped her glasses back on, giving them a quick tap up onto the bridge of her nose. "I'm sure you'll be fine. Like I always say, Lumberjane scouts are made of strong stuff."

Jen walked over to the scouts, pleased to find them where they were actually supposed to be. For the moment.

"Jem!" Rosie trumpeted, clapping Jen on the back. "How are you? Good day?"

"It's Jen," Jen corrected, smiling back. "And yes, thank you, it's been a real humdinger of a day."

"New badges for all your scouts," Rosie continued, as though she hadn't heard. "A good day I would say, Jeanette."

"Jen," Jen repeated, raising an eyebrow. "It's always JEN."

"All right, scouts," Rosie said, adjusting her glasses, "much to do, the day is young, much to do."

And she turned and marched out of the mess hall.

CHAPTER 9

Dinner was over. The scouts cleared their tables, washed up, and headed into the world of nighttime. Outside, the air was dusk mauve.

As April, Jo, and Mal went back to the cabin, Molly took a moment to stand under the stars.

Little lightning bugs looped around, flashing bits of green in the night, like dizzy flashlights.

Molly wandered past the fire pit, past the volleyball courts, into the forest on the edge of camp. She didn't go far, just along the edge of the tree line, so she could still see the cabins but feel a bit apart from them.

It wasn't that Molly took these walks because she missed being alone; that was actually a pretty crappy part of being at home, sitting in her room by herself, playing solitaire, reading or doing homework. Mostly doing homework. Molly's parents were obsessed with this idea that she wasn't doing well in school. Or well enough. Molly's parents were pretty convinced she wasn't doing well enough at a lot of things.

Molly pressed her hand against the bumpy bark of a big fat pine tree. Pine trees are amazing because like most trees, they really just do not care about stuff like homework. They just are.

Molly loved camp, and being with everyone—it was just sometimes she needed a moment to breathe. To feel space around her. To feel a tree.

"Hi there, tree," Molly sighed.

The lights in all the cabins were almost all off. Molly imagined all the Lumberjanes curled up with books, their flashlights glowing. She could hear the fabric of the Lumberjanes flag flapping in the breeze.

It was nice being with all the campers, feeling like a part of something, even when it was just a lot of people getting ready to sleep.

There was a rustling.

Molly turned.

A crouched figure waddled through the trees, snapping twigs in its path.

Molly squinted, waiting for her eyes to adjust to the soft light of the moon.

It was Bearwoman!

Bearwoman wasn't Bearwoman's actual name, and it wasn't a name she liked, but since she wasn't willing to tell the Lumberjanes her real name, that was what she was called. Mostly because in addition to being a grouchy old woman who wore thick layers of bulky coats, Bearwoman sometimes transformed into an actual bear, a big brown grizzly bear, to be specific. She appeared in camp sometimes, but it wasn't always clear from where. Or where she went when she disappeared. Also, as she'd often told them, it was none of their business.

At the moment Bearwoman was in human form, an old woman with a face that looked like it was carved out of wood, a pile of black and silver hair knotted on the top of her head, spectacles as thick as pop bottles perched on her nose, and what looked like turtle-shell kneepads. Bearwoman's face always looked like someone had just told her something really annoying.

Molly stepped forward into Bearwoman's path. "Hey," she said politely. "Nice evening."

Bearwoman looked around, as though considering this idea. "Good as any other night," she muttered. Molly, along with Mal, had actually had some adventures with Bearwoman, not that you could tell by the way Bearwoman talked to her whenever they ran into each other.

Tonight was no exception. "What are you doin' out here? Shouldn't you be in bed? That camp director of yours jus' lets you all go willy-nilly where you please in the middle of the night?"

Molly shrugged, "No. I just . . . I was just going for a last-minute but very short late-night stroll."

Bearwoman rolled her eyes and pushed past Molly. "Stroll," she grumbled. "STROLL. Ha! In my day, a Lumberjane had no time for strolling no way. When I ran this camp, there was no strolling at all! There was walkin' and runnin' and that was it! STROLL! A likely story."

Molly looked at Bearwoman curiously. "Where are you going?"

"None of yer business," Bearwoman barked. "I got stuff to do and it's nothin' to do with you or any of you all."

"Oh, I—"

"So bug off." And with that, Bearwoman shifted; in a puff of sparks, her shape twisted into the tall, furry, lumbering bear shape of her other form. As a bear, Bearwoman was as big as a house. Or at least a small cabin. She slammed against a tree, shaking down a hail of pine needles, and galumphed away.

Molly smiled. There was something about Bearwoman, something so cool. She was, like, this crabby old woman who could do and be whatever she wanted. It sounded

pretty awesome to Molly. Plus being able to turn into a bear!

Of course, Bearwoman wasn't the only one wondering what Molly was doing out in the woods.

"Hey." Jen stepped forward out of the dark, her telescope case hanging off her back. "What are you doing out here, Molly?"

"Oh," Molly said, suddenly flustered, suddenly aware that she was walking around alone in the woods like the beginning of a horror movie. "Just getting some quiet time."

"Excellent! Now we can all get some quiet time. In the cabin. Let's go."

CHAPTER 10

By the time Jen and Molly got back to the cabin, Ripley was fast asleep, making a snoring noise that sounded like a big fuzzy cat purr. Mal was reading a comic book, Jo was trying to read a book on quantum physics, and April was sitting on Jo's bunk talking about Rosie.

"You just KNOW, right, like everything Rosie tells us, there are like a million other details she leaves out."

"There's an entire encyclopedia of stuff we don't know about Rosie," Jo agreed, not looking up.

April was an avid collector of stories about Rosie. Like the story of that time when Rosie was a scout and she maybe possibly rescued a family of centaurs.

"I bet you when Rosie was a scout, she discovered a new creature every day. I bet she discovered a whole menagerie of new and mysterious beasts. I bet whatever I can think of, she's done it."

Jo flipped a page of her book. "That sounds exhausting."

"But cool!" April noted.

"But pretty cool."

April curled up in a little ball of April deep thought, her arms clasped around her knees.

"Why is it other people's bunks are so comfy?"

"Science," Jo said.

"Hmmm."

"You know," Jo added, dropping her book on her lap since reading was clearly not going to happen, "*we've* had some kick-butt adventures. And today, we found unicorns. So . . . pretty adventurous."

April nodded. "Oh, I know. I mean, yeah, totally we have."

"And who knows what we'll find tomorrow? We could stumble on another dimension on our way to breakfast, given our track record." Jo was fine with this, as Jo was not really all that into breakfast.

"That would be pretty wonderful." April sighed.

"As long as it's not a watery dimension, I'm good," Mal added from her bunk.

"Okay," Jen said as she opened the door, and Molly scooted inside and jumped onto her bunk, where Bubbles was already curled up and fast asleep.

"Lights out. Flashlights only." Jen switched out the light and dropped onto her bunk, content, for the moment, that everyone was in one place (where they were supposed to be, even!) and safe.

April dropped down onto her bed and curled up under her fluffy covers.

Molly slipped under her covers and whispered, "Good night."

"Good night," Mal whispered back.

"Good night," Jo called to the cabin. She leaned down so her head was hanging over April's bunk. "Dream about amazing things," she said.

April nodded. "I will."

CHAPTER 11

The next day was a whir that started with a breakfast of fresh-baked scones and then poured out into a day of Lumberjanes hardcore getting stuff done!

Barney and Ripley took off after breakfast to tap dancing class, in the new Lumberjanes dancercise studio, taught by the funky and flexible Mrs. Penelope P'Tattatattat.

Jo headed to the workshop to take apart various pieces of equipment and then put them back together to form new and astounding inventions (she also had to check on her vases that had recently come out of the kiln, in order to complete her View to a Kiln badge).

Mal and Molly were taking their second try at their Peace and Quilt badge, although Mal was getting a little sick of sticking her thumb with a needle every fifteen seconds.

"I am not a pincushion, I am a person!"

Then they were facing off against Woolpit cabin in volleyball doubles.

April was on her way to the library to grab some maps when Rosie spotted her from the porch of her cabin. "Hey there!" she hollered. "Come in here and lend me a hand?"

It took April less than two and a half seconds to get to Rosie's porch. ZIP! "How can I help?"

"I need a scout with steady hands." Rosie adjusted her glasses. "Game?"

April gave a sharp nod. "No problem."

Inside, Rosie's cabin was a comfy but very robust room full of books and other stuff both recognizable and cryptic. The room was actually a mishmash of tastes: baroque stuffed velvet chairs with gold frames—fancy filigree frames—mixed with flowery curtains and Rosie's own taste for plaids and heavy rustic furniture (most of which Rosie made herself). There were bookshelves up against every wall, stuffed with books and also boxes, some padlocked, and one secured with several locks and chains, which glowed faintly.

On one wall hung Rosie's impressive and diverse ax collection, which ranged in size from splitting hairs to splitting trees. One ax was currently wedged into the top of Rosie's desk, the biggest piece of furniture in the room. The desk was covered in wood shavings and a mess of wires and springs, topped with an old, curled-up piece of parchment with a gooey-looking red wax seal.

It's like a mystery sundae, April marveled.

Behind Rosie's desk was a series of portraits of the former camp directors, who ranged in style from stiff and colonial, with high collars and big hair, to scruffy and covered in little bits of forest.

Miss Qiunzella Thiskwin Penniquiqul Thistle Crumpet, with her thick mane of black curls piled on top of her head like a soft-serve ice cream cone, looked out imperturbably from her portrait, her sharp green eyes focused on April. Every time she visited Rosie's cabin, April spent a moment memorizing its incredibleness for future reference.

Rosie strode over to the far wall, her thick boots shaking the floor slightly, and grabbed what was actually a giant carving of a cat-like face with huge sprawling antlers as long as April.

Rosie picked up the carving and handed it to April. "Just hold 'er against that wall for me for a second."

April raised the carving above her head and leaned it against the wall. "Here?"

"Yup!"

April looked up. "What is this?"

Rosie seemed to consider the placement for a moment before answering. "A beast that's not to be tangled with.

Especially after a long rain. Or a rough artistic interpretation thereof. Which . . . I'm going to hang right . . . there."

Pulling a massive silver peg from under the handkerchief holding down her thick red hair, Rosie closed one eye, concentrating on her target. "Hold still."

With keen accuracy, Rosie tossed the peg, like a dart, threading the small loop at the top of the carving and embedding it into the wall.

Rosie stepped back, pleased. "Perfecto!"

April stepped away. The wooden creature swayed slightly on the peg, its eyes diamond shaped, its lips curled up in a satisfied smile.

"Thanks for the assist!" Rosie called out, as she headed into a back room off the main cabin. "I'm sure you've got tons to do!"

April had tons of questions for Rosie, about whether the carving of the creature was to scale and where it lived and all that, but Rosie was busy so . . .

April froze. There, hanging on the wall, next to a comfy chair covered in books and blankets, was a pair of green Lumberjane sashes. Sashes. Covered. In. Badges.

"Oh my GOSH," April breathed, reaching out to touch the faded edge of a sash with a careful hand.

Here, slung on a wooden peg over what looked like a raincoat, was every possible accomplishment a Lumberjane could earn. I mean, probably it was. There were so many! Rosie even had the bronze, silver, and gold double-ax badges, which were super hard to get, and . . . April blinked. What was that?

"It's the Extraordinary Explorers medal," Rosie said, returning with a silver bucket. "For extraordinary exploratory skills. They engrave your names on the back too. Kind of nifty."

April flipped the medal over. It was heavy, made of something that felt like rock but looked like gold. There, engraved in fine lettering, were the names Rosie and Abigail.

"That's—"

"Looking pretty good up there," Rosie said, nodding at the wall with the carving as she grabbed her ax. "All right then! Lots to do!"

And with that, Rosie scooted April out of the cabin and strode off to go wherever it is someone like Rosie goes with an ax and a silver bucket. "Thanks for the help, scout!"

"The Extraordinary Explorers medal," April whispered. It felt like every word linked together in a perfect chain. April leapt off the steps and ran all the way to the library.

CHAPTER 12

The sun was shining. April had the whole day in front of her. By Lumberjane standards, that meant anything was possible.

By lunchtime, April was hunkered down at the picnic tables with handfuls of maps, a compass, her notebook, and a modest mass of snacks.

April had spread the maps out over the table with the help of a few rocks. The thing about maps is, there's never just ONE map, not even of a single area. One of the spread out maps was a more recent map that showed all the different elevations around camp. One was a more old-timey-looking map that had a bunch of drawings of little trees where the forest was and little fish swimming in the lakes and rivers. Another map showed the various wildlife, with different dots representing different animals.

Plus April had her *Lumberjanes Flora and Fauna Guide* map, with its weird diamond pencil scribbles done by who knows who.

All around her, the camp bustled with Lumberjanes doing what Lumberjanes do, but April barely noticed as she pored over the maps, tracing Roanoke cabin's steps through the woods, over the stream, to the meadow of Clow Bells.

After two granola bars, an apple, a juice box, and a bag of potato chips, one thing was clear: The mountain they saw the day before wasn't on any of the maps.

The maps did show the forest they'd run through, the babbling brook that Jen fell into when she went looking for them, and the meadow of Clow Bells. But in every map, on the edge of that meadow was . . . nothing.

Not nothing, obviously, although that would be interesting, but no mountain.

A MASSIVE mountain just . . . not there?

April squitched her face up in deep thought.

No mountain. OR. A mountain that no one knew about.

April could feel her heart beating faster, the way your heart beats faster when something amazing is about to happen.

Because your heart is the first to know.

Maybe it meant no one had ever climbed it before? And if no one had ever climbed it before, that meant that this was an opportunity to be . . . an extraordinary explorer!

April sprang up from her picnic table and galloped, through a flock of Lumberjanes doing tai chi, over to the workshop.

The closer she got to the workshop, the bigger and better the idea felt inside her, like a burst of light that starts out sparkler big and a few moments later it's a firecracker, that starts out like a good idea and a few moments later . . . it's the best plan anyone ever had.

Of course of course of course! April thought.

The mountain!

CHAPTER 13

JO!" April called as she crashed through the doors, flooding the dusty workshop with light. "JO! GUESS WHAT?"

Flipping up her welding mask, which looked very cartoon villian and intimidating, Jo switched off her blowtorch. "What?"

"Extraordinary!" April hopped around the workshop. "And it's going to be awesome."

"Great," Jo said, leaning back against the giant metal table in the middle of the shop, prepared for this to take a while, "That doesn't really make sense, but when you've caught your breath, I'm all ears."

"Okay okay okay." April was so excited it was hard to

talk or stand still or both of those things at the same time, so she jogged in place in the workshop, in front of Jo, for a bit, saying, "Okay."

"Okay. Okay. Okay so . . . okay."

April closed her eyes; she could see the mountain in her mind's eye now, as clear as anything. She pictured herself gripping the side of the rocky face, the wind in her hair.

AND! When they got their Extraordinary Explorers medals, they could all have their names carved in them!

It was perfect. It was Lumberjanes-errific. It was probably even destiny, since what else do you call something you get to by way of UNICORN CHASE?

THAT'S DESTINY, BABY!

"Okay," she said again. It was hard to think with all these voices jumping up and down in her head.

Jo removed her gloves, familiar with April's moments of "OH MY GODDESS, GUESS WHAT?!" She probably even had time to go get a quick drink of water before—

April shook her hands out. "Okay."

"Whenever you're ready," Jo added. "Really no rush."

"Okay." April stopped moving. Possibly finally out of okays.

"You know the oath we took when we became Lumberjanes?" she asked.

"Obviously I do," Jo said.

April and Jo put their hands on their hearts: April on her sweater and Jo on her leather welder's apron.

"Once again with feeling, because I'm the only one who has it memorized . . . I solemnly swear to do my best," Jo said, pressing a leather glove over her heart. "Every day, and in all that I do . . ."

To be brave and strong,
To be truthful and compassionate,
To be interesting and interested,
To pay attention and question
The world around me,
To think of others first,
To always help and protect my friends
~~[illegible]~~
And to make the world a better place
For Lumberjane scouts
And for everyone else.

THEN THERE'S A LINE ABOUT GOD, OR WHATEVER

"Tomorrow," April said, hitting her palm with her fist, "we are going to go back and climb that mountain!"

"Which mountain?"

"The one from yesterday! By the unicorns!"

"Oh, right! Any particular reason?" Not that there needed to be a reason, Jo was just curious.

April put her arms up in the air, fingers outstretched, reaching toward the stars. "Because it's there but I can't find it on any of the maps." Holding up the maps she still had squished in her hand, she added, "Because there's this medal that Lumberjanes get when they do something extraordinary and Rosie has one . . . I mean she has all the badges but she has this medal too and when you get it they engrave all your names in it and if we climb a mountain that's not on any maps that no one has climbed . . ."

Sometimes there is just too much to say and not enough oxygen to say it.

April's cheeks glowed pink.

"Well," Jo said, thinking as she spoke, "I do have some new equipment I want to try out."

April punched up into the air. "Yes yes yes!"

Jo watched April, who was now actually jumping up and down with excitement. There was a speed to April's speech that made Jo, who knew April very well, realize that this thing April was excited about was something she was going to do no matter what. It was no-matter-what big now. Mountain big.

Back in the regular, non-camp world, in April's regular house where she lived with her dad, April's room was full of trophies and ribbons and medals. Jo once slept over at April's and spent the whole night transfixed by her walls of medals for skiing and arm wrestling, her trophy for chess, her gold cup for high jump, and her black belts for karate. In the regular, non-camp world, some of April's classmates called her an overachiever, which is another way of saying "intense," which is another way of saying "too intense."

Jo knew that April wasn't an overachiever, or too intense. She was someone who got an idea in her head, like winning the Mermaid Magic Fan Fiction Contest, or solving a mystery, and then she did it.

Jo also knew April long enough to know that her mom, when she was alive, was the same way. When she was alive, April's mom attacked the day in a way that made everyone exhausted but April.

April was someone who was only really being herself when she had a big idea in her heart that made her talk real fast until she was out of breath.

Jo didn't think that was a bad thing.

"Okay then," Jo said, picking up her welding equipment so she could put it away properly, because that was something that made Jo, Jo. "I'm in. I'll just get my stuff ready while you convince everyone else that it's a good idea."

April rubbed her hands together. "No problem!"

CHAPTER 14

April had to wait until after dinner, mushroom meatball night, to convince Ripley.

Actually, it was even longer than that because they were showing a Famous Female Directors retrospective after dinner, which was packed and also chock-full of films that made really interesting character choices.

By the time April, who was pretty much exploding with her awesome idea, got to her, Ripley was crashed out on her bunk after a night of movie popcorn and movie chocolate chip cookies and movie milkshakes and Nora Ephron.

"How do you feel about another round of unicorn and then a gigantic mountain climb tomorrow, Rip?" April asked, her words mashing together in her excitement.

Ripley was tucked in tight with her stuffed unicorn, Mr. Sparkles, wedged under her chin.

"Mmmmm, unicorn," she mumbled, turning over in her bed. "Yeah, let's unicorn."

"Excellent," April said, with a little fist pump. She turned to face Jo, who was standing by her bags with a twist of rope in one hand and a metal-looking thing in the other. "Okay, Ripley's in."

"Yeah. Let's unicorn dance," Ripley continued groggily, kicking off her blanket. "Turn up the music. Hey! Those aren't your tap shoes. Gimme those! Doughnut."

"I don't know if that's an actual yes, given she's clearly talking in her sleep," Jo noted, coiling up a very very long rope.

"Let's call it a definite maybe," April said, walking out of the cabin. "Two to go!"

"Guess what we're doing tomorrow!" April said, vaulting over to Mal and Molly, who were sitting at a picnic table getting Band-Aided up after quilting day.

"Uh," Mal said.

"We," April said, "drum roll, please, are going to go climb the mountain we saw by the unicorns yesterday!"

"Wait," Mal said, squinting as though she were trying to picture it but having great difficulty. "We're going to climb a mysterious, supertall, and probably very perilous to climb mountain?"

"Absolutely." April bobbed her head vigorously.

"Hmmmm," Mal said, "interesting. So. That sounds pretty dangerous."

April considered, her voice getting higher as she spoke. "Would I call it dangerous?"

"Um, it sounds at least a little risky," Molly proposed. "You know, not dinosaur dangerous but at least a little dangerous."

Dinosaurs being an 8 out of 10 on the average "How dangerous is this?" scale.

"And we're doing this why?" Mal raised an eyebrow.

Molly waited to see what April would come up with.

April always came up with something!

"Because it will be transcendent!" April trumpeted. "Because there isn't no mountain too high for a Lumberjane!"

"I'm pretty sure that's not the original lyric." Molly scratched her chin. "I think it's supposed to be—"

"Because Jo has a new invention she wants to try out." April interrupted. "Also there's this thing called the Extraordinary Explorers medal, which we would totally get if we manage this stupendous feat, which we can totally do because FRIENDSHIP TO THE MAX!"

That was at least three very solid reasons, April reasoned.

Over at Zodiac cabin, the members were practicing their accordion for their That's Accordion to You badges. The music switched from polka to something of a modern interpretation of polka, providing what could be described as the perfect soundtrack for the excitingness of the adventure to come.

Mal wondered what it would be like to spend your evenings not plotting to do dangerous things. You know? Just hangin'? Chillin'? Mal wondered when was the last time Roanoke cabin was chillin'. No memory came to mind.

"Fine," she grumbled. "At least we're not diving into a lake."

"I'm in too. I bet Ripley's excited to see the unicorns again," Molly said.

"Yes yes yes!" April cheered and then skipped back to the cabin to pack for their next adventure. There was so much to do! What did Rosie say? Be prepared! Something like that. Okay, so there were snacks, and a change of clothes in case it was cold at the top of the mountain, and more snacks to pack.

"Jo!" she called, flinging the cabin door open. "Everyone's in!"

On the picnic bench, Mal turned to look at Molly, who was enjoying the feeling of the night air on her face.

"If I could bottle a cool night breeze for keeping forever, I would," Molly sighed.

Sometimes Mal wished she felt the same way as the other girls seemed to feel about doing dangerous stuff like this. Sometimes when everyone else was getting all excited, she just felt nervous, or weird. Not that there was anything wrong with weird. I mean, Mal was fine with weird. Mal knew that most of the best people out in the world were weird.

Just . . .

Why did everything have to be weird and kind of life-threatening?

Mal looked out into the deep, dark woods. "Seriously, though. Is it me," she queried, "or are we always doing stuff like this? Like vaguely scary kind of crazy stuff."

"At least this time we're *planning* to do weird crazy stuff," Molly said, "instead of doing something crazy because we're being chased by something or because we fell into something or because someone is being held hostage by a god and needs to get saved."

"This time," Mal muttered.

"This time," Molly agreed, lightly swatting a mosquito away from Bubbles, who was snoring a bit on her head.

Mal poked at the rip in her jeans.

"Hey," Molly said, "we're all in this together no matter what. Right? As long as we're all together, it's going to be okay."

Mal stood up and stretched. "Fine," she said. "In the meantime, I'm going to get a pre-bedtime pastry."

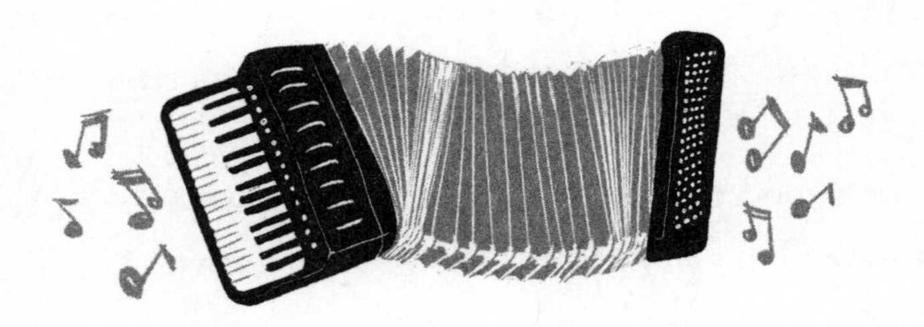

CHAPTER 15

Mal wandered back to the mess hall, where the stash of muffins could be found in the secret fridge behind the regular fridge, as anyone who has ever done KP (which is kitchen cleanup) knows.

As she passed Zodiac cabin, Wren, the only member of the cabin still sitting on the steps, stopped playing her accordion, which let out a final soft weeeeeze. Wren blew the purple hair out of her eyes. Wren's fingers were covered in rings she had made for her May the Forge Be with You metalsmithing badge. Mal noticed she was also wearing a vintage Le Tigre T-shirt, which, you know, good band.

"Hey!" Wren called. "You play music, right?"

For a bunch of reasons that were both kind of obvious and weirdly unobvious, Zodiac and Roanoke cabin didn't always get along. Although Barney was a Zodiac, and everyone at Roanoke loved Barney. Mostly, though, Zodiac were still mad because of the small matter of Diane, who was once a member of Zodiac and also, possibly, a Roman goddess and who was involved in a mystery that Roanoke kind of solved, which also resulted in getting Diane kicked out of camp for a bit.

Mal paused. Then nodded. Twisting one of the rings in her ear, she replied, chill, "You guys were playing really good."

Wren sighed, dropping her chin on her accordion. "We kind of suck."

"What the Cyndi Lauper? You guys are totally great!"

Wren held up the accordion. "Well, we have an extra if you want to play with us."

Mal pointed at herself, dubious. "Play with *me*?"

Wren frowned. "We need someone who can read sheet music. Hes is the only other one who can, and she's not really into it . . . Can you? Read sheet music?"

"Oh yeah, totally. My mom and my grandma are musicians. My grandma is a flutist, and she taught me when I was little."

"Can you play the accordion?" Wren's accordion was bright red with flames painted along the sides, and shiny black keys and buttons.

Mal grinned. "No," she said, "but I play the guitar, the tuba, the clarinet, the drums, the violin, the piano, and the flute, obv, so . . . how hard can it be?"

Wren rolled her eyes. What was it with Roanoke being good at doing, like, so many things?

"Okay," she said, standing and putting her accordion back in its case. "We're practicing tomorrow night before dinner."

"Excellent," Mal said, in a voice that only thinly disguised her total and utter excitement. It would be so great to play something again. It was kind of weird not playing music for so long, really, because that was pretty much all she did back home.

Even when she was a little kid, she would go to her grandma's house every day and practice the flute while her grandma fought with her cats over stolen socks.

Maybe Zodiac would start a Lumberjane band! Maybe she and Molly could be IN the band! Or Roanoke could start a band, in between adventures . . .

Mal waved good-bye and trotted back to the cabin. Because sometimes when you get a really awesome idea in your head, other ideas like muffins get shoved out your ear.

That night, in Roanoke cabin, after teeth were brushed and all the flashlights were out, everyone dreamed.

Technically, everyone dreams every night, but sometimes those dreams are particularly awesome.

Molly dreamed about Bearwoman, stalking through the woods.

Jo dreamed about the basic mechanics of pulleys.

Ripley dreamed about unicorns.

Mal dreamed about making kick-butt music for a roaring crowd of screaming fans.

When April, who was up long after everyone else, finally fell asleep, she dreamed about the mountain.

PART TWO

GET ON UP BADGE

"Summit in the air"

All Lumberjanes aspire to achieve great heights, and mountain climbing is just one way to access high places. As mountain climbers, Lumberjane scouts must use their knowledge of knots, ropes, and the basics of gravity to surmount the mountain face. Like any endeavor, tackling a mountain of any size—even traversing a molehill—requires planning, careful footwork, and, above all, teamwork.

Mountain climbing teaches Lumberjane scouts the importance of concentration, application, and caution. Note that at the summit of every mountain, a Lumberjane must remember that what goes up . . .

CHAPTER 16

The Lumberjanes have a long and proud herstory of adventuring, as well as peril, mystery, and encounters—wrestling matches with the seemingly impossible.

Encountering and accepting the challenge of the impossible are pretty much what Lumberjanes do. They are reckless and brave.

Which is to say, being a Lumberjane is always a little bit about destiny.

Lumberjanes know well that tickly, cold, big-punch feeling of destiny, like a big bite of ice cream, except it's a big bite of ice cream to the heart.

The next day, April woke up and bounced out of bed like a gymnast springing off a vault.

As her fellow Lumberjanes slumbered, April watched the sky turn from nighttime purple to morning yellow and blue. Of course, Jen was already up and out getting stuff done, because Jen was up even before the sun crept up over the horizon. Today, Jen had her camp counselors meeting, which was so super early it wasn't even a morning meeting, it was a dawn meeting.

It was going to be a perfect day, April thought. She could feel it in all her bones: the little bones in her feet and her fingers, the Lego blocks of her spine, everywhere.

April stood on her bunk and reached up to give Jo, whose bunk was above April's, a poke in the shoulder. "Hey!" she whispered loudly. "Jo? Jo! You awake?"

"Clearly not," Jo said, face down in her pillow. The cover of the thick book Jo was currently reading, about molecules and other small things, peeked out from under her pillow-case.

"Okay, well." April rested her chin next to Jo's pillow. "You're going to wake up soon, right? Because when you get up, we can get the show on the ROAD."

"Mmmmhmmm." Jo pulled her covers up tighter. At home, Jo's dads had invented an alarm clock for her that woke her up by quizzing her on basic quantum physics.

April was much louder and more persistent than this alarm clock.

Also, April did not have a snooze button.

"Okay, so," April said, jumping down to the cabin floor, "we've got to make our bunks, go for breakfast, get snacks. So that's maybe thirty minutes. Which means we'll have plenty of time if we can all RISE AND SHINE IN THE NEXT FIVE MINUTES!"

"WHA?!" Jolted awake, Mal sat bolt upright in bed, her one awake and open eye staring at April. "What time is it? What's happening?"

April had already tossed on her shorts and a crisp, clean shirt and was slipping on her shoes. "It's time to wake up!"

Jo stepped down from her bunk, finding a path on the floor that wasn't covered by yesterday's sweatshirts and sweaters and socks and . . . oh, a granola bar.

Taped to the door, in Jen's impeccable handwriting, was a list of things "FOR ROANOKE TO DO" for the day.

Jo grabbed the list off the door. "Hey, we've got a lot of stuff to do today," she said. "I'm guessing cleaning up the cabin is one of them aaaaaaand . . .Yes it is, item #42, 'Clean Cabin.'"

April grabbed the list and shoved it in her pocket. "We can do it when we get back," she said, quick quick. "Plenty of time. No problem."

"All fifty-three items?" Jo queried. "Oookay." She went back to her bunk to get dressed. Jo's clothes were not among the piles of clothes on the floor. Her khakis were neatly folded in her drawer.

Ripley's clothes *were* all over the floor.

"Mmph," Ripley slithered out of bed, crept across the floor like a caterpillar, and twisted into the T-shirt lying on the floor next to her bunk. After a few minutes of wriggling, her head emerged through the neck hole. POP! "Pants. Socks. Breakfast," she murmured. "Doughnut."

Bubbles the raccoon was still curled up in Molly's morning hair, which looked like an artful blonde bird's nest. "Ooooo. Definitely doughnut." Molly yawned, stretching in the coziness of her sleeping bag, which she was pretty sure was the coziest thing in the universe. "Has anyone seen my socks?"

Outside, the horn section of the Lumberjanes' get-out-of-bed brass ensemble blasted the opening bars of Joan Jett's "Bad Reputation."

"Look at them," Wren grumbled, peering through the window of Zodiac cabin as Roanoke marched to breakfast. "Do they even SLEEP?"

Roanoke was the first cabin in line. Roanoke was in line before there even WAS a line of scouts waiting for breakfast. Breakfast was not doughnuts but a healthy meal of muesli, bananas, and fresh-squeezed orange juice, prepared by the scouts of Roswell cabin, working on their Sound of Muesli badge.

Mal stepped up and grabbed her bowl off the counter.

"Is it me," she mused, "or is there a badge for every culinary occasion?"

"It's not you," Molly said. "I'm getting my S'more the Merrier badge next week."

"Barney told me they're getting their Gourmet It Over With badge! They're making FONDUE!" Ripley cheered.

April was so excited she could barely think about food.

The camp counselors were all sitting at a table in the corner, already knee-deep in their Counselor Brainstorm Session, which is basically the meeting where counselors talk about stuff the campers are doing and what to do about it. Also it's the meeting for figuring out who has what duties, like moose stall maintenance and KP. The counselors were all in their green and yellow uniforms, their little green berets all perched perfectly on their different-shaped heads.

Maddy, the counselor for Woolpit cabin, had just finished discussing the upcoming volleyball tournament, which the members of Woolpit, who were all really into sports, were hoping to totally and completely DESTROY. Jen was at the head of the table, taking minutes. Which was something she liked doing. Jen particularly liked the part where she got to say, "Let's bring this meeting to order!"

At Roanoke's table, April was bringing breakfast to order,

which meant making sure everyone ate a lot and very fast.

"All righty!" April shoveled two giant spoonfuls of grains into her mouth, chewing speedily. "Let munching commence posthaste!"

"Jeez, April," Mal groaned, "how about letting a girl finish her orange juice?!"

"No time!"

Ripley pushed a few extra spoonfuls of muesli into her cheeks. Bubbles jumped off Molly's head and did the same.

Jo finished her juice and slipped a few bananas into her pack.

Molly munched her muesli and wondered what Bear-woman ate for breakfast. Maybe fish?

The day was already getting away from them! April thought. She jumped up from the table and started ushering everyone out. "Let's go, let's go, let's go!"

Rosie, carrying a giant sack of who knows what, was stomping in just as the scouts of Roanoke were charging out the door.

"In a rush?" Rosie inquired, dropping the sack on the ground with a giant THUMP. She peered down at Ripley's bulging cheeks. "Storing up for winter?"

"MUFLI!" Ripley pointed to her cheeks.

Bubbles gave a muffled squeak.

"Just eager to get out and revel in the beauty of the great

outdoors," April gushed, wrapping her arms around Ripley.

"Excellent!" Rosie said, picking up her bumpy-looking sack and resuming her path into the mess hall.

"Is it me," Jo wondered aloud, "or is Rosie always carrying something that is just a little mysterious?"

Jen didn't notice the scouts of Roanoke come or go in the mess hall, in part because they came and went so fast and in part because as they were leaving, Jen was knocking on the table and calling out, "Let's bring this meeting to order!"

"Jeez," Marcie, the head counselor of Dighton cabin, fumed, "we've come to order four times in the last ten minutes. Can we get a move on?"

Standing outside Roanoke cabin, April was ready to move. While everyone else got their bags, she paced. The buzz she had from this morning was all over her body now: She could feel it in her nose and her hair and her toes and her small intestine. It was excitement! It was time! April jogged in place, her pack bouncing. "Onward!"

Ripley and Bubbles were the first to bounce out the door. They jumped in the air in a tandem starfish formation.

"UNICORN!" Ripley cheered.

"SQUEAK!" Bubbles squeaked.

"WE'RE OFF!" April hollered.

And so they were.

CHAPTER 17

Finding a herd of unicorns the second time around required a bit of fancy footwork and retracing of steps, which was tricky because, as Jo noted, unicorns don't leave footprints.

"Isn't it hoofprints?" Molly asked, as they made their way through the first round of trees and forest, following the map from the flora and fauna guide.

"Maybe it's tracks," Molly continued, as they carefully stepped across the Babbling Brook, balancing on the few stones poking above the water's surface. "Unicorns have tracks, right?"

Mal cautiously stepped over a bit of brush, still keeping an eye out for vines and other possible predators, of which there could be infinite numbers just waiting for an ambush.

You really never knew.

Molly listened to the crunch of the forest floor under her feet. Nature's carpet, she thought. She imagined having big paws and feeling her claws dig into the damp forest floor as she ran.

Just then, Molly felt a small tug on her foot. Dropping down on one knee, she thought she saw, just for a second, a tiny green sliver twisting through the pine needles on the ground. But it was only for a second.

"Molly?" Mal stopped and looked back, pushing her black hair out of her face. "You okay?"

"Yep," Molly called forward. She stood and jogged up to Mal. It was probably nothing, she thought. Bubbles, waking from a brief nap on Molly's head, chirped excitedly, and bounced off to chase after a butterfly.

"Don't get lost," Molly called.

"The forest smells so lusciously foresty today," Ripley said, twirling after Bubbles.

"Enjoy it while you can," Jo noted.

"Hey," Mal said, once Molly caught up, "guess who got invited to play accordion with Zodiac cabin?"

"You?" Molly guessed.

"Yeah! I haven't played anything in so long. I hope I don't suck." Mal was practically hopping, she was so excited.

Maybe she could play one of the songs she wrote back home? Molly would love it. Hey, it could be a surprise!

"You're going to be awesome! What are you talking about?" Molly pushed her hands into her pockets. "So. I mean, you'll be practicing a lot with Zodiac, then?"

Mal nodded vigorously. "I mean, I'm in a band at home, right? We practice all the time. I mean, that's practically all I do at home. My mom always says you gotta practice if you want to get good. Before she was in a band, she played guitar since she was, like, six. Which SHE did because my grandma was obsessed with practicing. She practiced like eighty hours a week or something!"

Molly bit her lip. It was dumb, obviously, to feel a little bit jealous about someone you cared a lot about finding something they liked a lot that wasn't something you were going to do together.

She shook her head, trying to shake loose whatever thought was hitting the bottom of her stomach. It was silly.

"Hey," Molly said, kind of quietly, like just above the sound of the crunch of their feet on the ground, "do you ever think of the ground in the woods as nature's carpet?"

Mal was already thinking about accordion band names. "Hey, we'll be back in time for my practice before dinner, right? I mean, we can't be gone all day and all night, right?"

"Sure," Molly said quietly. As she stepped forward, the small green thread, slightly vine looking, clung to the heel of her sneaker.

CHAPTER 18

April forged ahead, eyes, shining like high beams of determination.

A day with a plan was always a good day. The feeling of possibility was invigorating, like the few cups of coffee she'd tried over the past year: a jolt to the brain.

The night before, lying on her bunk, while everyone else was snoring, April sketched the mountain, from memory, into her notebook, currently tucked in her back pocket.

Because it was from memory, it wasn't a very detailed sketch. Mostly it was just a jagged line going up, then a little bit down, then up and up and up into the clouds, then down the other side. All around the mountain, she drew little stars (and a few unicorns for good measure).

On the back of the page, April could see her drawings of other creatures and things from their adventures: the three-eyed Brontocreatures, the two-headed centaurs, and the elephant-headed Grootslang.

April had been keeping notebooks like this since she was old enough to hold, instead of try to eat, a crayon.

April actually came from a long line of women who made extensive lists of the things they were going to do and then did them. April's mom said they came from a "can" and "will" family, not a "should" or "might" family.

When April finished drawing the seventh star around her mountain, she drew a picture of the Extraordinary Explorers medal. Rosie's was embossed with an image of a pair of binoculars over a set of crossed oars, all circled with a line of tracks with an X marks the spot at the top.

And on the back would be all their names: April, Jo, Mal, Molly, and Ripley.

April stepped out of the tree line and felt the sun on her face.

On the edge of the grassy meadow, Mal breathed in deep. Then went a bit green.

"Well," Molly coughed, covering her nose with the sleeve of her shirt, "here we are."

"UNICORN CITY!" Ripley squealed, jumping up and down.

"Wow, is it possible it's even smellier today?" Mal wondered.

Still grazing the fields of abundant Clow Bells, the rave of unicorns seemed to be in an energetic mood. A few were munching but many of them dashed around the meadow, in tight circles and then larger loops; like skateboarders skidding around the edge of an empty swimming pool, they hit tight curves, zinged in one direction, then turned and zinged back in the other.

Their tails fanned out behind them like streamers as they swooped, bending the Clow Bells lightly beneath their feet.

"What's that sound," Mal wondered, stepping closer.

"What sound?" Molly asked, stepping up beside her.

"It sounds like . . . ringing? Like wind chimes or something. I wonder where—"

"Unicorn dance!" Ripley sang, twirling toward the unicorns.

Jo and April stood among the whooshing unicorns and looked at the mountain. It was pinker than it was before, like a ballerina's tutu with a dash of cherry Popsicle, or bubble gum with a splash of strawberry milkshake. It was a color that brought to mind a lot of things that would make a person hungry, if you thought about them too much.

April grabbed her notebook from her pocket and a pen from her knapsack. She wrote, "Pink," next to the mountain, making sure their great adventure was well documented.

"Documenting?" Jo mused, looking over April's shoulder, which was not hard because she was so much taller.

"It has that je ne sais quality to it." April sighed, waving her arm dramatically in the direction of the mountain. "Doesn't it?"

A sliver of a chill rippled through the air. As April slung her knapsack around to grab a sweater, her notebook dropped to the ground. "Also it kind of changes color the more you look at it. The MORPH you look at it."

"It's Light Coral HTML #F08080," Jo joked, leaning her head back as far as it would go without its falling off. She added, "You really can't see the top. It's all covered in cloud."

"Between those rocks there," April pointed. "That's our way up."

"All righty," Jo smiled.

The plan was unfolding perfectly.

"All the way to the top!"

Jo reached down to grab Bubbles, who was bouncing up and down with his arms stretched upward. "Hey, where's Mal and Molly? Where's Rip?"

CHAPTER 19

While April and Jo were looking at the mountain, Ripley and Dr. Twinkle, who seemed to remember Ripley from two days before and walked toward her as soon as she appeared, were having a unicorn connection, which went something like this:

"Hello, Dr. Twinkle," Ripley sang sweetly, taking a single tiptoe step toward him. "How are you today?"

Dr. Twinkle soundlessly stomped his foot and shook his purple and gold mane. His silver horn flashed in the sunlight.

Another tiptoe step. "Did you miss me?"

Dr. Twinkle dropped his head down, his forelock curling around his horn and falling over his face. He pulled out a Clow Bell from the ground and started munching it.

"Well, I missed you," Ripley whispered. She twisted the arm of her sweatshirt, loosely tied at her waist, around her finger. "I missed you a lot."

Dr. Twinkle finished munching and seemed to nod his head even deeper this time.

Ripley took three more tiptoe steps toward Dr. Twinkle, then cautiously put her hand on his neck. The smell wasn't so bad, really. Ripley had smelled worse. Actually, there was this one time Ripley's mom's dog got sprayed by a family of skunks. That was a little worse.

Dr. Twinkle dropped his head again and pulled another Clow Bell from the ground, clumsily dropping it in Ripley's palm.

"For me?!" Ripley squealed. She threw her arms around Dr. Twinkle's neck. "Thank you!"

Meanwhile, several steps away, Mal and Molly were making their own discovery. Just past where the unicorns grazed, steps toward the beginning of the mountain, where the ground stopped being covered in grass and became dusty soil, was a pile of pink and purple rocks. There were a lot of rocks, really, scattered here and there, getting bigger and bigger, from the size of a bowling ball to the size of a small person, the closer they got to the mountain. They were made of a material that looked to Mal like quartz, like the crystal Jo sometimes wore around her neck.

It looked like maybe the unicorns had knocked some of the piles over. There were bits of wood scattered too, wood that had worn and weathered until it was powdery and gray.

Sticking out of this particular pile of rocks, face down, was a sign. An old sign, maybe even older than the archway over the entrance to the Lumberjanes camp, made out of a long piece of wood with jagged edges on both sides.

Molly reached over and gently tipped the sign up so they could read the text. "Huh," she said.

There was something about the sign, to Molly, that had a quality beyond a regular sign. Maybe it was just that this sign was old and old signs feel important, because the stuff that they're pointing at has been there for so long.

Mal looked at Molly. "What do you think it means?"

Molly shrugged. "I don't know. I mean, you think that's . . . the name?"

"HEY!" April called, marching over, fully charged and ready to go. "Let's go! The mountain awaits!"

"This Mountain," Molly said, matter-of-factly.

"Right!" April tightened her hair bow and rolled up the sleeves of her pink sweater determinedly. "This mountain. We're going up *this* mountain. Today! Now, even!"

Jo, who had retrieved Ripley, who was pretty unicorn blissed out, stepped up to the group. "We're ready," Jo said.

Bubbles squeaked approvingly from Molly's head.

"Molly was just saying," Mal explained, "that we think this is This Mountain."

Ripley leaned forward, a slightly limp Clow Bell tucked in her pocket. "WHA?"

Molly pointed to the wooden sign, which did in fact read, THIS MOUNTAIN.

"Hmmm," said Jo.

"EXCELLENT," said April. "This Mountain it is. Ready?"

"Ready."

"Ready!"

"Yep."

"Sure."

And with that, they trooped off toward the mountain.

Ripley turned and waved one last good-bye to the unicorns. "GOOD-BYE, UNICORNS!"

"Come on, Rip!" Jo called back.

"COMING!" Ripley skipped past the pile of pink and purple rocks, over other pieces of gray wood that could very well have been more pieces of sign—but who has time for signs when there are mountains to conquer?

CHAPTER 20

An ancient Chinese philosopher, Lao Tzu, once said that a journey of a thousand miles begins with a single step. That's not exactly what he said, but it's close. Actually, there are probably a lot of people who have said something similar over the years, because it is true.

Mal was thinking it might actually take them ten thousand steps to get up This Mountain.

April was not thinking about steps or miles. For April, the objective was clear: Get to the top of the mountain. Victory dance. Return and collect super amazing Extraordinary Explorers medal.

Victory dance.

Behind the sign was a small path, which was not a path so much as it was a narrow gap where a single person could walk through a series of giant rocks shaped like giant bowling pins, snowmen, and other basic rock shapes, all made of some sort of purple and pink rock.

Jo stretched her hand out and felt the rocks as they passed. They felt cold, like ice cubes almost. Which was weird because it was a pretty sunny day.

At first, the route twisted back and forth, then it stretched out like a steep runway, and then it curved up and around the mountain base.

The scouts moved into single file: April, then Jo, then Ripley, then Mal, and then Molly.

Jo scanned her surroundings, a habit, as they walked. The climb itself was a little disorienting; it was hard to see which way they were headed, other than, obviously, up. Initially, it seemed like they were on one part of the mountain; then they came around a curve and the rocks around the path parted, and Jo realized they were headed in what seemed like the completely opposite direction. The sun blazed overhead, high in the sky.

"This rock is very odd," Jo pondered aloud, looking down at her feet as she walked. "First of all, it doesn't seem to absorb heat. Second, you'd think if someone else had been on this path, some of the rock would be broken up, and it's not."

April looked down. "It looks like it's carved out of ice."

Jo nodded. "It's like the mountain, This Mountain, is one solid rock."

She smiled, reaching out to run her fingers along the rock. "It's a mountain unlike any other!"

Jo rubbed her chin. "I just hope my climbing equipment works. Normally, I would anchor my ropes between rocks, but I don't know if we can do that. Everything seems smooth and solid. No cracks anywhere."

"We'll figure it out." April stopped and turned to give Jo a playful punch in the shoulder. "We always figure it out! Remember that time in the canoe with that three-eyed monster thing? The time we were in the cave and you used the Fabio series to get us over those pillars?"

April swiveled and continued up the path. "We got this!"

"I don't know . . ." Jo considered, recalling a moment in their adventures when she was teleported to a very gray and weird alternate reality for a brief but unsettling period. "We DO seem to have a knack for getting through tough things. Using, among other things, the FIBONACCI series."

"Right," April nodded, increasing her pace.

Jo rolled her eyes. No matter what, though, April was her best pal, and best pals are there to back up best pals. It's a thing. Like a secret handshake, which April and Jo also had.

Mal looked back at Molly. "Hey. What do you think April would say if we had to turn back early so I could go to band practice?"

Molly shrugged. "I don't know," she said. "April's not really the 'turn back early' type."

"Yeah," Mal said, "but we could always come back—"

Jo, April, and Ripley had stopped. In front of them was a steep face of rock, higher than a house. Like a waterfall of frozen pink lemonade. Now the path was straight up.

"Whoa," Ripley said, "how are we gonna do this?"

"With Jo's new invention!" April said, confidently holding up a metal spike and a long length of rope.

"Fingers crossed," Jo admitted.

"Oh goody," Mal groaned. "Crossing fingers."

CHAPTER 21

April, who was the strongest climber, volunteered to be the one to free-climb up the sheer face first. Free-climb means no ropes holding you in case you fall.

So not falling is a big part of free climbing.

"The hardest part will be getting up and making an anchor somehow," Jo said, running her hand over the smooth rock. "If you see something at the top, like a tree, something solid, you can tie the rope to that."

"I'm knot worried," April said.

Jo raised an eyebrow.

"Knot is spelled K-N-O-T," April added.

"Got it," Jo said, placing a coil of rope and her invention in April's pack.

"Wait, what happens once she gets up there?" Ripley asked, touching her chin to the rock so she could look all the way up.

"Once April gets up, she's going to secure an anchor so we can suspend a rope for us to climb up." Jo held up a small metal contraption with little holes cut into the sides and a small set of interlocking gears. "Then she's going to use my new invention to help her pull us up the rock face. It's a self-pulling pulley," she explained, moving her arms in a way that suggested she might be trying to mime exactly what the pulley would be doing. Except it mostly just looked like she was milking an invisible cow.

April bent down to tighten the laces on her spiky shoe covers, or crampons. "I'll whistle when everything's secure."

April stood up, steadied herself, and then turned to the wall of rock. She reached up with her left foot, found a toehold in a tiny divot in the mountain surface, and pulled herself up to the first handhold she could find.

"You okay?" Jo asked quietly.

"Yep," April said. "I'm feeling BOULDER than ever!"

"Okay then," Jo said. "Any more mountain puns?"

"Not at the moment." April squinted, spotted the next toehold, swung her foot up.

Rock climbing was one of April's favorite birthday activities, especially at Lillian's Indoor Rock Climbing Bonanza, just outside the suburbs where she lived. April loved the focus of it: reaching from one handhold to another, up and up, until you hit the top—and the feeling of hitting the top was pretty awesome too. The woman who ran the place, whose name wasn't Lillian but Dragon, was never not in climbing gear. She used to let April stay an extra hour.

At Bonanza, she wore a harness.

April pressed her lips together. There was no harness now, and no room for doubt.

This climb was super steep. Maybe a lot steeper than April had bargained for, especially given there were almost no real places to get a grip. There weren't any cracks in the rock, but there were tiny folds, just enough for the very tips of April's fingers and the edge of the blades on her shoes. One by one, she found the little piece of grip she needed to get herself up.

Mal whistled. "That is really really steep," she said.

"Yup," Molly said.

"You can do it, APRIL!" Ripley called up.

The rock was slippery. It didn't feel grainy like other

rocks April had climbed. It felt like glass. April grabbed another tiny fold and pulled.

Okay, she thought. April, you can do this. There is only can and will. There is only can and will.

With every pull and grip, April repeated this sentence.

"There is only can and—"

April felt her foot lose its grip and skid along the side of the rock. All her weight dropped into her right hand.

Before she knew it, a high-pitched "EEK!" escaped from April's lips.

"APRIL!" Jo called up, her voice sharp with worry.

"It's okay," April called back, shakily regaining her toe grip. "I'm okay!"

I can do this. I will do this.

April reached her hand up and felt, with the tips of her fingertips . . . a ledge.

I can do this. I will do this. I can do this.

With all her might, she hoisted herself up and over the edge of the rock face.

"I DID IT!"

The air was crisp. It was really cold. Icy. April looked around. The mountain felt bigger up here. Wider. Through a light mist, she could see more pillars of rock, ghostly in the light mist of fog.

Jo was right: It was going to be hard to anchor the rope.

April turned. There were two tall peaks of rock that seemed solidly embedded in the ground, not too far from the edge.

Dragon always said two anchors were better than one.

April tied a rope around each rock and then slipped the two ropes into Jo's gadget.

Then she leaned over the edge of the cliff and whistled to Jo.

Jo looked up and whistled back, just as the rope appeared.

"Okay," she said, turning to Ripley, "you're first. Molly, why don't you let me take Bubbles?"

Ripley bounced over to the rope and gave it a light tug. "BEAM ME UP, APRIL."

April turned the seven interlocked gears of Jo's self-pulling pulley.

CLICK! CLICK! TING!

Down where Ripley and Jo were standing, the rope started incrementally inching its way back up the mountain.

Jo leaned forward. "Actually, you still have to climb a little . . ."

"COOL!" And with that, Ripley planted her feet on the face of the rock and, hand over hand and with the help of Jo's rope gadgetry, pulled and was pulled up to April.

CHAPTER 22

It would have been a pretty strenuous climb without Jo's invention, which turned the rope into a sort of conveyor belt.

Jo, who was also a pretty avid climber, went last. Just in case someone needed help.

"That was really slippery," she said, when she finally grabbed April's hand at the top. "I really don't think I've ever seen a mountain like this."

Once they were all up the face, a group hug was clearly in order.

April squeezed her friends ferociously. "Crackerjack, we're awesome!"

Ripley, who really really loved a group hug, wiggled happily. "YAY!"

Mal looked around, wide-eyed. "It's like a whole other world up here," she said. It felt alien. Pluto-like. A place where earthlings dared not tread. The air felt like it was Air Lite. Air Free.

Molly stood at the edge, for a moment, and looked down at the now tiny unicorns below. It was hard to see them because of the fog. They looked like the Dippin' Dots her mom liked to get at the mall.

Ripley pulled on Jo's arm. "Why is it so foggy?"

Jo looked around. "Fog happens when cold air meets warm air," she said. "We must have hit a colder spot. Probably because we're getting kind of high up."

"Cooooool," Ripley exhaled and watched as the phantom of her breath mixed with the fog.

April coiled the rope and slung it over her shoulder in case they hit another steep part. "Okay," she said, pointing to the gap in the rock where the trail continued, "upward!"

Everyone started walking except Mal. "Uh. Hey, so, just asking, but when do you think we'll be back?"

April turned. "I don't know. I mean, the plan is to get to the top, and we don't know exactly how long—"

Mal's eyes darted to the side. "Do you think we'll be back before dinner?"

Jo shifted her backpack. "Why?"

"I have . . . an appointment to practice the accordion

with Zodiac?" Mal said, her voice uncertain. "Before dinner."

"Okay, but we have a plan." April's face did a small crumple, like a little fold in a crisp piece of paper.

"Yeah," Mal said, hopeful, "I know, I just . . ."

Molly, Ripley, and Jo looked from April to Mal and back.

"Sure," April said, a little unsure. "Once we finish this."

"Okay," Mal said.

"We're almost there!" April cheered, switching gears to let's-get-up-this-mountain mode. "I can feel it!" And with that, she turned and started hiking again.

"Stay close," Jo called back, as Ripley scampered behind her.

Mal walked a little slower than a scamper. Molly watched Mal's shoulders hunch. Like she was bummed. Like she didn't even want to be hanging out with them.

Molly felt a little drop in her stomach. The fog swirled like soft serve in increasingly thick layers, so it was harder and harder to see.

Molly could feel . . . something.

Something? Something . . . not weird. But . . . something.

CHAPTER 23

Back at the mess hall, Jen was feeling pretty good about her counselors' meeting. They got a bunch of stuff done. Made plans for repairs and for various duties that different cabins would take on. Initial organization for the upcoming Intergalactic Space Fanatics Convention (which is what they were calling it, maybe that wouldn't be the final name) was also starting to take shape.

Now she just needed to check in with Rosie.

Great. Jen's shoulders sagged ever so slightly, like someone had just placed a small sack of flour on her back.

Jen stepped up to Rosie's private cabin. Stood up straight, pushed her shoulders back to Jen position. Jen knew (because her mother taught public speaking skills) 80 percent of the success of a transaction like this was attitude.

"Your name is Jen," she whispered to herself. "Your name is Jen and you are a capable, responsible camp counselor."

Jen leveled her little green beret. Next to Rosie's door, an angry raccoon statue, recently carved from the trunk of a massive pine, bared its teeth.

Jen turned and bared her teeth back at the creature. Then she straightened and knocked twice on the door, hard.

"COME IN!" Rosie hollered from inside. "DOOR'S OPEN!"

Jen took a deep breath and stepped inside.

"JANET!" Rosie's voice had the force of a small freight train.

Rosie was seated behind her desk, which was covered in scratches and marks from where she'd stuck her ax in there for safekeeping. Although some of the marks on the desk did look distinctly claw-like. One corner looked like someone, or something, at some point, had taken a bite out of it.

A really big bite.

Jen leaned forward. Wait, she thought, is that a tooth still IN the desk?

Rosie was enjoying a mug of chamomile tea and was working on what looked like a large wooden clock. A clock that seemed to have at least four minute hands.

"What is that?" Jen asked. "And it's Jen, just, by the way. Jen."

"Oh, just a little piece of gadgetry, something to keep track of things, you know," Rosie said, carefully sliding a metal wire into one of the many keyhole shapes in the box and twisting it with her fingers. There was a blue spark and the wire disappeared. "Damn."

Jen shook her head. Not knowing what Rosie was talking about seemed as normal as the weather. "We're almost done organizing our next round of camp activities," she announced, voice level, firm, confident. "The counselors are really excited—well, I'm excited, with the lunar eclipse coming, to talk about some celestial things with the scouts. It's going to be great."

"Excellent." Rosie looked up. "I'm sure you have a handle on it, Jinni. So what are your scouts up to today?"

"Oh," Jen nodded efficiently, unfaltering, "it's Jen, and they have a list of things they need to get done. I'm sure they . . ."

Jen paused, with a feeling not unlike the feeling you get when you start to slip on a patch of ice. No, they probably weren't, were they? They were probably doing something they weren't supposed to be doing. "Oh, uh. I'm just about to check on them," she blurted.

"Oh, they're smart scouts," Rosie said, turning back to her strange clock-like contraption, which was glowing green now. "What did they do the other day? Oh yes," Rosie looked up. "Living the Plant Life!"

Jen tapped her clipboard, suddenly anxious to see what her very smart scouts were up to. "Yes. They found . . . um . . . Clow Bells, and unicorns," she added.

Rosie dropped the second wire she'd unwound from one of the larger spools on her desk. She raised an eyebrow. "Unicorns?"

"Oh," Jen waved her hand, "I mean, yeah, when I found them they were with these unicorns, next to a large . . . mountain, I guess? Anyway, I should get going."

Rosie adjusted her glasses. Unicorns and Clow Bells, she thought, with a slightly concerned "hmmmmm." Unicorns and Clow Bells. What was it about Unicorns and Clow Bells? And a mountain? Something. Possibly something worthy of some level of concern.

Rosie stood up and grabbed her ax from its spot wedged in her desk and her moose bridle from its hook on the wall. "Jen, I think you and I should go find your campers."

"Well, it's J—. Oh. Yes. Really?" Jen's eyes grew wide. "Why? Is everything okay?"

"I'm sure it is," Rosie said, tossing the bridle over her shoulder. "But let's just go check to be sure."

CHAPTER 24

The path up the mountain continued to twist to the left and the right, getting steeper and steeper, like it was pulling up and away with every step.

Meanwhile, the fog was getting soupier and soupier. Ripley focused on keeping Jo's head in her view. Fog swirled around them, painting the air so that everything was soft white and hard to see.

Molly focused on the purple women's symbol patch sewed onto the back of Mal's jacket.

"This seems dangerous," Mal said, possibly to herself. "Right? Like I know I say this a lot, but we can't even see our own hands in front of our faces."

Ripley pressed her hand up against her face. "I can see MINE," she yelled back. "But it's like RIGHT UP ON."

Mal groaned, pressing to keep up. "We're going to lose each other."

Molly looked down. She couldn't even see her own sneakers, just her knees and the swirl of movement of each of her steps.

"APRIL!" Molly called out. "Mal's right, we need to SLOW DOWN!"

Bubbles squeaked nervously, wrapping his tail tighter around Molly's head and grabbing her ears with his little paws.

Jo reached forward for April, touching her lightly on the shoulder. "April. This fog is crazy."

April frowned. It wasn't crazy, it was just thick! Fog was thick! That's why they called it fog!

April swiveled, squinting as Jo stepped into view. "It's fine!" she said. "We'll clear the fog and we'll be able to see."

Jo shook her head. "I think maybe," she pressed, "we should turn around."

"Turn around?" The thought of it was like a red light blinking behind April's eyes. TURN AROUND? Did turn around mean STOP? It did. STOPPING would be . . . would be . . . UNEXTRAORDINARY!

That was it exactly, April thought. We can't turn around! We're extraordinary explorers! Sure, there were people in this world who turned around when things started seeming impossible, but April was not one of those people. Rosie would probably NEVER turn around because of FOG.

"We can come back tomorrow," Jo offered. "Maybe we just need a day with better weather."

April threw her hands up. "We're so close!"

Jo stopped walking. "April."

April shook her head. "We just need . . ."

April stopped. Jo paused. Ripley froze.

April felt something. Like her foot hit something gooey. Or soft. Or like instead of standing on a mountain, she was standing on mud, or Jell-O, or muddy Jell-O.

Her foot. Was sinking. Slipping backward.

Jo's eyes went wide. "Whoa," she said, "did you feel that?"

April wrapped her hand around the rope on her shoulder. "I think so," she said, cautiously.

April's foot sank a little farther.

"What's happening?" Ripley whimpered, pulling one foot up, then the other.

"Hey, guys!" Mal called. "Are you there? What's going on? It feels like—"

And there was a sound.

Like a whoosh? A skittering like the sound icy snow makes in the wind.

"Did you hear that?" Mal asked.

"What?" Molly said, stepping forward and, she hoped, out of whatever she was sinking into.

"Whoosh," Mal said.

"Whoosh?" Molly asked.

Mal tilted her head. "Like the sound snow—"

"GUYS!" April screamed.

April grabbed Jo who grabbed Ripley who grabbed Mal who grabbed . . .

"RUN!"

CHAPTER 25

April scrambled up the slope. Jo grabbed Ripley by the back of her shirt and starting running with her like she was a human suitcase.

It felt like they were running in a dream, arms and legs moving, going nowhere. It was impossible to tell if they were moving, because all they could see was fog. It wasn't even fog anymore. Just a sea of solid white filling the air.

"WHAT'S HAPPENING?" Ripley hollered, her voice shaking as she was jostled in Jo's grip.

The ground. It was like when you try to run up a sand dune, Jo thought. It felt like it was slipping away.

"The rope!" Jo called to April.

April grabbed the rope off her shoulder and tossed an end down to Jo.

Jo made a few loops in the rope and tossed it back to Mal and Molly. "GRAB ON!"

Mal scrambled to get her footing, with Molly scrambling behind her. Mal spotted the rope and lunged forward, arm outstretched to snatch the loop as it swung through the air. Not that she could see anything. The rope landed on her palm just as she stretched out her fingers.

Mal closed her hand, gripping tight. "I got it!"

As Molly's feet continued to sink into what used to be the rock of the mountain, which was now clearly something else, she felt something curling its way around her ankle. Something twisty. "AUGH!"

"WHAT IS IT?" Mal yelled back, twisting the rope around her wrist so she wouldn't lose it.

"My leg!" Molly reached down to slap whatever it was that was now curling its way up her calf. "There's something on my leg!"

"WHAT?"

"I DON'T KNOW!"

April tied Jo's contraption to the other end of the rope, her hands shaking. Good thing she had her My Fair Lasso badge. If she threw the rope upward, maybe it would catch on something? Maybe they could . . .

April could hear Mal and Molly yelling, and she could feel Jo and Ripley puffing behind her.

April flashed to the first time she tried knitting, which was something on a list long ago, and she dropped a stitch and then the whole sleeve she was working on just . . . came apart.

That was the perilous thing about knitting, it can go from a sweater to a ball of mess in a matter of seconds.

Makes you wonder why so many people think knitting is "relaxing."

Which is not to say April didn't finish her sweater eventually.

All the cold air of adventure drained out of April's body, and her head got hot with fear. What if something happened? What had she gotten her friends into?

April frowned. Nothing's going to happen to my friends, she thought. No way, not on my watch. NOT HAPPENING.

Gritting her teeth, she tossed the rope, with Jo's metal contraption on the end, in the air, swung it in two wide arcs, then she whipped it up as hard as she could and . . .

April felt the rope thread through her fingers as it sailed.

Up?

And?

CHICK!

The rope hit something and then . . . went taut.

Okay, April thought, Jo and Ripley are tied on, so are Mal and . . .

"MOLLY!"

Mal had stopped running, spun around, and was reaching back, the rope twisting tight around her wrist as she held her free hand out to Molly.

"Grab my hand," Mal cried. She could barely see Molly's face, her eyes wide, for the fog.

There was a moment where she felt Molly's fingers hit her fingertips, once, and again as Molly tried to get a grip on Mal's hand. "MOLLY!"

"What's happening?" Jo called down. She couldn't see a thing.

"I can't reach," Molly gasped. She couldn't run because it felt like there was nothing to run on, her feet circled in the air. She reached one more time, grabbed at the tips of Mal's fingers.

And just as Molly's fingers slipped out of Mal's grip, something snaked its way up Molly's calf, along her side, and across the palm of her hand.

CHAPTER 26

"It's just this way." Jen's voice bounced and wavered as she shouted against the wind. She was perched behind Rosie on the camp director's favorite moose, Jeremy. One hand on her beret, one hand around Rosie's waist, Jen gripped Rosie's flannel shirt for dear life. "To the left!"

Jeremy was a fine riding moose, the pride of Rosie's stable, with antlers as big as canoe paddles, but even a fine riding moose is not an ideal ride for two. Especially when galloping through the woods.

"You saw this mountain WHEN?" Rosie hollered back at Jen.

"Day before yesterday," Jen considered. "Is there some special mountain stuff I don't know about?" She grumbled to herself, "Not that there aren't a million mystical things around here no one ever tells me about."

"What's that?" Rosie called back, her voice steady and loud in the whistling wind.

"I said what is it about the mountain?" Jen called forward.

Jeremy snorted, not really enjoying people yelling while on his back.

"There's a story," Rosie said. And she pulled on the reins and Jeremy ground to a halt, right before he ran into a field of unicorns. "It's an old story, so I'm not sure I'm remembering it correctly. But it's about a mountain near a field of unicorns."

"What's the story?" Jen said, dropping down from Jeremy's back and into the field of Clow Bells.

"Like I said," Rosie said, rubbing the fog off her glasses, "I can't quite remember it."

"THIS story you can't remember!? Of all the stories, THIS story is evading you?"

"Well, there are a lot of Lumberjanes stories to remember," Rosie reminded her, shoving her glasses back on. "I remember most of them."

Jen's eyes went wide with frustration.

Rosie looked around. "Just give me a minute."

There was a distant rustling sound. The rave of unicorns stirred.

"Man, that is a strong smell," Jen coughed, covering her nose.

Rosie sniffed and wiggled her nose. Yes it was. "Smells like the toe jam of an ancient seafaring Monolusky," she noted.

"Whatever that is," Jen said.

The unicorns were all stepping forward and circling around to see who the new moose was. Moose don't mind the smell of unicorns, so Jeremy was pretty much fine with this. He snorted appreciatively. Held his head up high to show off his cool antlers.

One unicorn whinnied as if to ask what the moose was doing there.

Jeremy snorted back that he had no earthly clue.

Just then, Rosie felt something grabbing onto her foot. She bent down and looked carefully at the little green threads working their way onto her boot.

"Well, hello there," she said, "little clinging thing."

"What is that?" Jen asked, walking over. "Is that poison ivy? Wandering vine?"

"Nope." Rosie held up the little green vine for Jen to see. "This," she said, "is a very clingy and sometimes useful thing called Clingy Vine."

CHAPTER 27

Clingy Vine grows in places where a person might find any bell-type plant, also wherever you find berries or baklava. It likes attention and tall grass, and it is not in any way poisonous, or edible. If you see Clingy Vine, it's not necessarily a bad thing, but it can be inconvenient if you are not into the idea of having Clingy Vine around, or if you're trying to keep your shoes clean.

Clingy Vine can be a useful thing, because in addition to clinging onto you (to your shoes, shirt, and so on), it can also reach out and cling onto other things.

So it's actually a very useful thing in very stressful falling situations.

When Molly's hand slipped from Mal's, the Clingy Vine that had wrapped itself around Molly's ankle and leg and waist grew. It twisted around Molly's right arm and across her open palm, dove off her fingertip, and landed on Mal's left hand. It crawled across Mal's hand to her wrist, where it twisted itself around and around, threading a bridge between Mal and Molly.

And just at that moment, the rope that was holding Jo, April, Ripley, Mal, and Molly received what could be described as a tremendous tug.

"AAAAHHHHHHH!!" the Lumberjanes hollered in unison, because what else could be done at a moment like that?

Mal wondered if this was what it was like to be a yo-yo, and she decided never to yo-yo again.

Whatever was tugging on the rope switched from tugging to swinging. Yes, something, or someone, very big seemed to be swinging the rope.

Now, instead of plunging through a mysterious white fog, the members of Roanoke cabin were swinging back and forth through it.

Like a pendulum, Jo thought.

And then, suddenly, they were swinging up into the air, higher, higher . . .

"AAAHHHHHHHHHH!!!!" everyone screamed, because circumstances seemed to still indicate the necessity of hollering.

It was not unlike being on a swing set and swinging as high as a person can swing. Except the Lumberjanes were on a rope full of Lumberjanes, and they had no idea why they were swinging or why they were suddenly . . . hanging . . . in midair.

"WHAT IS HAPPENING?!" Mal, who now had her hand firmly gripped around Molly's, howled.

"HANG ON!" April screamed.

Gravity says you can only hang in midair for so long.

Sometimes, in some magical situations, gravity can be a little bit wrong.

But in this case, gravity seemed to be on point, and after a moment the Lumberjanes were falling.

Fast.

Of course, the good thing about falling is you can't do it forever.

PART THREE

The out-of-doors is just outside your door, whether you are a city girl or a country dweller. Get acquainted with what is near at hand and then be ready to range farther afield. Discover how to use all the ways of getting to hike over hill and dale, to satisfy that outdoor appetite with food cooked to a turn over a hunter's fire, to live comfortably in the open—all of these seem especially important to a Lumberjane. She is a natural-born traveler and pathfinder. She has an urge to get out and match her wits with the elements, to feel the wind, the sun, and even the rain against her face.

If you know how to lay and follow trails, how to walk without getting lost, how to build a fire that will burn, and how to protect yourself from the weather, and other more unnatural (or even supernatural) forces, your wits are likely to win in this matching contest. You need to practice outdoor housekeeping, in all its forms, before you can be a real explorer or camper.

I SAW THE SIGNS BADGE

"A sign of the times"

The world is a complicated place. Knowing where to go and where you are going is key to the success of any adventure. A Lumberjane knows that natural and human-made signs are there to help us get where we are going in one piece, and to ensure the safety of those around us. To achieve their I Saw the Signs badge, Lumberjanes must master crypto-signology, semiotics, symbolism, and signifiers. They must also know the basics of road signs, forest signs, lake signs, desert signs, and mountain signs, as well as hand signals and light signals. Do you know the signs? Do you know, for example, the first sign of . . .

CHAPTER 28

The Lumberjane scouts of Roanoke cabin fell from the sky and landed on whatever it was they were landing on in the following order: April hit the ground, bounced up into Jo, who was holding Ripley, all three of them hit the ground, bounced up again, and landed. Then Mal and Molly arrived in a twisted ball of vine and rope and landed on top of Ripley, Jo, and April.

"OOF!"

"OOOF!"

"OOOFF!"

"OOOOFFF!"

"OW!"

The heap of pink, plaid, green, khaki, and orange groaned collectively.

"Alive?" Molly called out from the tangled mass of Lumberjanes.

Mal took a deep breath. "Alive," she sighed.

"Yup," Jo said, stretching her legs out of the pile. "Definitely alive."

"ALIVE!" Ripley, who was tangled in a mass of rope, waved.

Bubbles jumped onto Molly's neck and wrapped his furry little arms around her. "Squeak!"

April's head popped up out of the pile of Lumberjanes. She threw her hands up in the air and yelped, with the relief of a thousand Aprils, "LUMBERJANE POWER!"

"Thank Gerlinde Kaltenbrunner," Jo said, shaking her head as she cautiously untangled herself from her friends' limbs.

"That was CRAZY," Ripley gasped, still squiggling in a mass of rope.

"That was definitely in the nut family," Mal groaned, standing.

Molly looked around at her fellow Lumberjanes, relieved. "It's a good thing to remember just how awesome it is not to be squished like a bug."

April spun around, taking it all in. "You guys! This is the top, right? WE MADE IT TO THE TOP!"

"We really need to work on our crash landing formation," Jo said, cracking her back. "Or not."

"Add it to the list," Mal grunted, testing out her feet to see if they still worked.

April grabbed Jo by the collar and shook her happily. "WE MADE IT TO THE TOP OF THIS MOUNTAIN!"

Not exactly as planned. But still!

"Ah yes," Jo chuckled under the wave of April's unbridled enthusiasm. "WOOO!"

"Yes, we did." Molly pulled herself up off the ground. "So where are we?"

"The top of the world. Holy Amelia Earhart!" April struck a victorious pose. "WE DID IT!"

It is a rare thing to feel like you're in the sky instead of having the sky above you. To literally be on top of the world, your nose pressed against the ceiling. April breathed in. Was this the highest mountain she had ever climbed? Yes! The air was sharp. A gentle mist, much thinner than what they'd climbed through, clung to the air, leaving a haze of sparkly, twinkly stuff in the atmosphere.

The rest of the Lumberjanes took a moment to look around.

Curiously, it didn't look like most mountaintops.

First of all, instead of the pink stone, now the ground under their feet was slightly spongy, and bumpy, like a carpet made out of a thousand snowballs, or like those art projects where you make snow by gluing a bunch of cotton balls together on a piece of paper.

Stretched out in front of them were little puffy hills and cotton candy wispy spires.

"Little help?" Ripley reached a free hand out from a giant hair ball of rope.

While April untangled Ripley for what was probably the two millionth time (because Ripley had this thing for getting tangled in string-like materials), Mal and Molly contemplated their own recent discovery.

"That was really scary," Mal breathed. "That was like some weird scene in some action-adventure movie or something."

"Totally," Molly whispered back. "I might not want to be an action-adventure star."

"No kidding."

"What happened?"

Molly held up her hand. Thin strands of green hairs still clung to her fingers. "Look." Molly twisted around, pulling her shirt out. They were all over her shorts, her shirt: little threads of green silk. "They're everywhere."

Mal turned her hand over, and the threads caught the wind and floated off her fingers like dandelion fluff. "Holy Beatrix Potter. What is it? Is this . . . a plant?"

Molly held a thread between her thumb and forefinger; the thread looped around and stuck back to the underside of her thumb. "Clingy Vine, maybe."

Most of the vine had snapped in the fall, or was floating away, but one or two fragile green threads were still holding Mal and Molly together.

"It must have grabbed me when you were falling," Mal breathed.

Molly's eyes went wide. "Yeah. Wow."

Mal grabbed Molly in a bear hug. "I'm never going to be weirded out by a plant again," she said. "Thank you, vine."

"Me neither, not that I was," Molly added with a smile, grabbing Mal's hands.

Mal winced.

"Wait. What's wrong?" Molly looked at Mal's wrists. The wrist with the Clingy Vine was fine, but the wrist that had the rope wrapped around it was turning a light shade of purple. "Oh no! Mal!"

CHAPTER 29

Mal bent her wrist and grimaced. "Maybe it's sprained?"

Molly called out, "Mal's hurt! CALL AN AMBULANCE! WE NEED BAND-AIDS STAT!"

All the Lumberjanes stopped and looked at Mal.

"WHAT?"

"OH NO!"

"MAL!"

"FULL MOON FORMATION!" April cried.

The Lumberjanes circled Mal in a cluster of concerned Lumberjanes.

"What happened?" April asked, kneeling in front of Mal, her eyes full of worry.

"I think it's from me wrapping the rope around my wrist when we were falling through midair and trying not to die," Mal offered. "Just a guess."

"Good guess," Jo said, her voice soft, bending over to look at Mal's wrist. "Who has their First Things First Aid badge?"

"Barney," April said. Really really wishing she had hers too.

Ripley raised a finger up in the air. TING! "I know how to treat chicken pox, because my whole family had it once, even my cat."

Mal frowned at her throbbing wrist. "Thanks, Rip."

"Like all my sisters and my brothers. Like all at once!"

Mal smiled a small smile.

"Do you want a hug?" Ripley offered. "That's actually the one thing you're not supposed to do when you have chicken pox, but I don't think that's what you have."

Mal smiled and nodded, and Ripley wrapped her arms around Mal in a gentle hug. Bubbles curled up in Mal's lap and raised his paws for a raccoon-style hug.

"Thanks, Bubbles."

"Well, I don't know first aid but I have sprained my wrist before. We definitely need to get you to a nurse or something," Jo said.

Molly put her hand on Mal's back. "We need to get back down to camp, pronto."

"Yes." April stood up. "Yes. Yes." She clapped her hands together. "Okay. Yes. Let's totally get down right away. Right! So!"

April put her hands on her hips, which is often the stance a scout will take when she is about to fix everything. Actually, standing with your hands on your hips is a very effective way to look and feel authoritative and proficient. April's face fixed into an expression of determination.

The plan was still in effect. Maybe not perfectly, she figured, but they got up this weirdo mountain. Now they just had to get down. Everything was going to be okay. All April had to do was figure out how . . . to get down. Right. Didn't plan that out exactly. Still. Totally fine.

Somewhere in this white fluffy place was a way down . . . Right.

April turned. The fluffy place was on top of a mountain, right? So . . .

April walked a few dozen steps away from the huddle of Lumberjanes, expecting to find . . . what? An edge? A sign of where the path was to get back down the mountain? A jagged edge of pink rocks peeking through the clouds? One of those things had to be around here somewhere, she thought.

But the puffy whiteness just unfurled. And unfurled and unfurled. It was like the first minute of non-snow right after a big blizzard, when you go out in your backyard and everything is just white. The slide, the swing, whatever it was you forgot to put in the garage, all blanketed in white.

Infinite, which is to say, endless.

Jo watched April turn to the left. Walk a few dozen steps. Turn to the right. Walk a few dozen more. Then she stopped.

"Uh," April said.

Jo walked over. "Uh?"

"Okay . . ." April paused and walked a few more dozen steps. "We're going to be fine and this is fine, I just . . . can't . . . find the path down."

"Oh, uh, hey, guys," a voice behind them said. "Welcome to Cumulous!"

CHAPTER 30

The voice belonged to a long-legged, long-armed, willowy creature with gray skin, long white wavy hair, and a long, flowing white beard framing a chubby, smiling, pearly face, round like a pug face if it were made out of full moon.

Next to the tall creature was another, slightly shorter creature with the same hair and face and a small gray knitted cap on top of its head. Both creatures wore long robes cinched at the waist in a style not unlike a bathrobe you might find in a fancy hotel or in the bathroom of someone who likes a nice bathrobe.

Actually, it was exactly like that.

The creatures smiled at the scouts with big pearly smiles.

"Hey, dudes," the first creature said, in a kind of gravelly, sleepy voice, giving a long, slow wave. "I'm Swish, uh, and this is totally Flap."

Flap peeked its hand out from under its robes and did a floppy wave at the scouts. Flap's voice was even more gravelly. And slower. "Yo. Cloudy, you guys!"

"Sup?" Swish grinned. "We're Cloudies and, uh, like I said, this is totally Cumulous so, you know. Cloudy!"

Swish and Flap glided forward through the swirl of whiteness, little white boots with puffy toes peeking out from under their robes.

"Hey, uh, Cloudy to you too," April waved, stepping up sharply. "My name is April and this is Jo, Mal, Molly, and the person hugging you right now is Ripley. We're Lumberjane scouts."

"Hey," Ripley said, her arms already wrapped tightly around Flap's fluffy robe. "Your coat is really fuzzy."

"Yaaa, thaaaanks," Flap nodded, patting Ripley on the head. "Your hair is totally sunny clear skies. I like the blue."

"April did it!" Ripley pointed proudly at April.

"So this mountain is called Cumulous," Jo looked around. "We thought it was called This Mountain."

"Oh uh, mountain? Uh no," Flap reached out its other hand and began combing its long gray fingers through the curls of its beard. "This whole place is called Cumulous. It's, like, a land above the earth, you know? It's really big, actually, we should probably give it more than one name, but . . . you know, we haven't gotten around to it."

"Yaaa. Dude," Swish chuckled. "we're totally raining off on that."

Jo looked around, the gears in her brain turning.

"Yeah so." Swish looked around. "That was pretty crazy back there with you falling. We were up here, like, you know, hanging out, having a super sunny tea party. And we heard you guys yelling, like, thunder boom crash, and we were like, 'WHOA. What the rain?' You know?"

"Yeah," Flap nodded. "So we, like, stopped and we were like, 'Dudes. That does not sound sunny!'"

"Then this rope, like, zoomed in like lightning." Swish said, its voice full of awe.

"And then Flap was like, 'Dude, we should pull on this rope, because, like, maybe it's attached to all the thundering boom crash,' right? So we did. We just pulled on the rope and then, WHOA, you guys flashed all way up there, and then you came back down. Now here you are! Rainy day about the rope."

Flap pointed to the frayed bits of rope next to their feet.

"Yeah," Jo said, looking down, "too bad, er, rainy."

"Did we rainy day your tea party?" Ripley asked, concerned, because that's a pretty bad first impression.

Flap waved it off. "Nah, dudes. We have so much tea. It's sunny."

"Okay," April nodded. "So we're super . . . sunny to be here but our friend is hurt. And we need to get back down right away. So can you let us know the best way to get back down the mountain?"

Swish and Flap put their hands up on top of their heads. Then they turned and pressed their foreheads together, which made a tiny clinking sound, and then they looked back at the scouts.

"Uh, rainy day. Like, not really," Flap said.

As they spoke, the mist around the Cloudies settled to reveal even more bright blue sky stretched in a dome shape around them.

Jo looked around. "Cumulous," she repeated to herself. "We're in the clouds. We're standing on clouds?"

Flap nodded, digging its hands into its bathrobe.

"Wait. And we can't get down?!" April yelped.

Flap shook its head. "Yah, dudes, I mean, if you wanted to go down . . . Wow, it's so rainy to say this but . . . you shouldn't have come up, right?"

"What does that mean?" Molly tightened her grip on Mal's shoulder.

"Well," Swish offered, "there were signs, right? On the ground?"

"This Mountain," April said.

"Foggy," Flap said.

CHAPTER 31

It didn't take Jen long to find the sign the girls had read earlier, perched in its pile of pink and purple soda-colored rocks.

Rosie was off circling the fields on Jeremy, looking for the girls, and Jen was investigating on foot. No sign of the girls. Then. The sign.

"This Mountain," Jen read aloud, her brow furrowed. "This Mountain what?"

There was very little Jen disliked more than a fragmented sentence.

A fragmented sentence isn't a sentence. At best, it tells you something a sentence could be about, if it had some verbs.

Jen looked around. Sometimes a verb was just something you had to look for. Spotting the other bits of wood scattered among the rocks, she stepped forward and started turning the pieces over. Some of the pieces were blank, some were so old they were almost not even wood anymore and crumbled in her hands like an old cookie. But many of them had more words inscribed into them: please, because, not, climb.

"Finally," Jen muttered. A verb!

After picking up as many words as she could find, Jen kneeled in the grass with an armful of bits of wood, verbs, nouns, and conjunctions, which she laid out in front of her in a wide arc.

"Okay, Jen," she muttered, twisting her long black hair into a knot, "somewhere in here is an actual sentence. All you need to do is find it." She began rearranging the sign pieces.

Word puzzles weren't really Jen's thing. Word puzzles were Jo and April's thing. Unfortunately, Jo and April were wherever it was they decided to go off to instead of doing what they were ASKED to do, which was a list of stuff that needed to get done around the cabin and the camp but . . .

Jen bit her lip. Her stomach churned. She KNEW something was wrong, she knew it. Her camp counselor instinct, well honed, was rarely wrong. Maybe never wrong. Or maybe it was just that Roanoke cabin was always doing something, and so her camp counselor alarm was always going off.

Which was very stressful.

Rosie galloped up on Jeremy. “They’re not here,” she said.

Jen looked at the sentence she had managed to puzzle out.

A sign.

A warning.

Rosie jumped down from Jeremy’s back. “Just smelly unicorns as far as the eye can see.” Rosie adjusted her glasses. “But I did find this.”

Rosie held out a small hardbound notebook. Grass stained the corner.

It had the words PROPERTY OF APRIL written with black magic marker on the front.

"When I found it, it was open to this page," Rosie said.

Rosie carefully opened the notebook to its last entry: April's picture of the mountain. "Seems likely that they came back for more than just the unicorns," Rosie said, closing the book and sticking it in her bag.

"It sounds like something they would do," Jen said, and bit her lip.

"Did you find anything," Rosie asked.

Jen nodded. "Look."

Rosie read the words at Jen's feet. "Hey, please do not climb this mountain. For a variety of reasons but mainly because it is not a mountain and it is stormy dangerous."

Jen stood up. Once again, she thought, the world was full of weird things she wished she understood or at least had some clue about in advance.

"The mountain," she said, pointing behind Rosie. "It's . . ."

"It's what," Rosie looked up.

"Gone!"

CHAPTER 32

"Okay, quick recap," April said, stabbing her finger into her palm, "Just. Okay. So. You're saying that This Mountain, this mountain we just climbed up, just now, like JUST NOW, doesn't exist?"

"This is rainy days." Swish seemed to be turning the words over in its head. "So, like, it doesn't exist *right now*."

"We were JUST on it," April repeated sternly, to ensure clarity, miming their ascent for the Cloudies in case she wasn't being clear enough. "We were climbing," she added, demonstrating, "with increasing effort." April lifted her legs up to indicate a strenuous ascent.

"And then we were like this, AAHHHHHH!" Ripley showed them falling so the story would be complete. "And then our friend's wrist got hurt."

"Blue skies. Totally blue skies. Except ya, the mountain's gone now. It might be back later, though," Flap mused, its hat sliding off its head slightly.

"What? That's nuts!" April threw her hands up. "That is just CASHEWS, man!"

"That does seem very unlikely to be true," Jo said.

But, Molly thought, not all that unlikely, given the many unlikely things that were always happening.

Mal flopped to the ground, cross-legged, and tried not to think for a second. Her legs felt like jelly.

"Well, like, it's a bit foggy?" Swish tilted its head and stroked its beard. "It's not like it's not there, just that a lot of the time, it's not there."

"Most of the time it's there and then it's not there." Flap's voice seemed unsure, or at least very laid back. "It's there and then sunny days and . . ."

"And then it's not there? It just disappears?" Jo looked at April.

April looked like her head was about to explode.

"Some of it does, sometimes all of it," Flap said, patting its cap, "Foggy, right? So that's why we tell people not to climb it. Because it could go at any minute so, you know, pretty stormy if you're on the mountain when it's not there, because, then—"

"Whoosh," Mal grumbled from the ground.

Flap looked around. "Uh. Whoosh isn't here right now, but Whoosh will definitely be at tea later."

Swish looked at Flap. "Hey," Swish said, "you know who they should talk to?"

"Oh yeah," said Flap, braiding its beard absentmindedly, "totally."

And with that, Swish and Flap floated off, their robe ties dragging through the light mist in their wake.

When Swish and Flap disappeared into the clouds, they left behind them a silence thicker than a triple strawberry gelato shake, extra thick.

Molly sat down next to Mal and gently took her wrist in her hand. "Hey," she said quietly.

Mal looked at her wrist.

Jo looked at April. Ripley looked at Mal and Molly.

"This is BONKERS!" April looked pleadingly at Mal. "There has to be a way to get down."

"We need a safe way to get down, because someone's already been hurt," Molly said, looking at Mal with concern.

Suddenly the hardest thing April had ever done was just stand still and look at her friends, who were all looking kind of scared and kind of mad.

"How was I supposed to know the mountain wasn't a mountain and we couldn't get up and be able to get back down, or even up?" April looked at her feet.

Mal looked at her wrist. Being hurt sucks.

Mal gingerly got to her feet and looked hard at April. "Of course we're on a mountain that's not a mountain. Because stuff like this always happens to us! Because we're always DOING this stuff! And now we're stuck up here. Maybe forever."

Ripley's eyes got big as saucers. "Are we?"

"Well, hold on," Jo objected, putting her arms around Ripley.

"This wasn't part of the plan!" April shouted. "I mean if I had known, obviously . . ."

April didn't know what else to say. All her words were balled up in her chest.

Mal didn't know what else to say either. Everything she wanted to say sounded kind of mean in her head, mostly because her head felt like it was splitting down the center.

So she walked away.

"Mal!" April's face twisted.

But Mal was already gone, holding her wrist and trying to hold back the tears that were already pouring down her cheeks so why bother.

Jo turned and looked at April, who also looked like she was about to melt into a tiny puddle of April. "We'll think of something," Jo said solemnly.

Molly ran off after Mal.

Ripley pulled the little Clow Bell out of her pocket and thought about a time when all they had to worry about was smelly unicorns.

Out of the mist, another figure, less willowy and not in a robe, emerged. "Is that a Clow Bell? Don't tell me you were hangin' out with those stinkin' unicorns."

CHAPTER 33

Jen and Rosie stood in the spot that had been a mountain but was now just a clearing past the fields of unicorns and Clow Bells. It looked like an empty sandbox, a patch of desert with just a few rocks here and there. A faint mist, like a few dozen *pffffts* of hairspray, hung in the air.

Here there was once a mountain. It seemed impossible. Now there was just Jen, Jeremy, and Rosie. And empty, inexplicable space. And Jen was freaking out, which involved a lot of arm waving.

"I was here the day before yesterday," Jen said. "I'm telling you, I was here and there was a mountain right here!"

"Yes," Rosie said, kneeling down and placing her hand on the ground, which was warm to the touch. "Hmmmm."

"And can I just say, SEEING A WHOLE MOUNTAIN is not something you make a mistake about," Jen went on, pacing in circles of increasing diameter, "and I know there are a lot of things to be wrong about. But this is a matter of MATTER!"

"Well," Rosie lifted her hand from the ground and looked at her palm, where the faintest layer of a soft pink dust glittered on her skin, "yes and no. Really, it's a matter of a mountain. Currently, it's a matter of how to get up a mountain that isn't there."

"Have you remembered the story you forgot yet?" Jen asked, exasperated.

"I have." Rosie looked around and breathed in the air to see if it was sweet or sour. Mostly it was faintly unicorn. "It's a story that takes place a long, long time ago, before one of many wars, about a scout, a very determined scout, who vanished, and was last seen headed toward a meadow of Clow Bells and unicorns." Rosie adjusted her glasses. "It was long before me. Long before anyone who's still on the council."

Jen clapped her hands on the side of her face. "SHE VANISHED?"

"She went to climb a mountain and she never returned." Rosie stood and looked up as far as she could look. All she could see was empty space. Empty space and empty space and empty space . . . and cloud. "POOF!"

"POOF!?" Jen threw her hands up in the air.

"I'm not saying she exploded," Rosie clarified, still looking up, because there was a story of a camper who had gone poof once, but it was a minor explosion and everyone walked away okay. "I'm saying whatever she climbed up, she never came back down."

Jen, who didn't know the story of the student who sort of exploded but ended up okay, was squeezing her head so tight it looked like it might go POP! "POOF!?!?"

Rosie put her hand on Jen's shoulder. "Breathe, Jen. We'll get them back. We just need to figure out how. Lumberjanes don't give up on Lumberjanes, or on mountains, or on mountain climbers."

"It's J—." Jen tilted her head, alerted to the sound of her actual name. "Oh. Right. Okay. Well. We better."

"We will." Rosie scratched her head, which was full of many thoughts. Mostly about how to get up a mountain that used to be there but now no longer was.

CHAPTER 34

"Who are you and what are you doing here?"

The woman standing in front of April, Jo, and Ripley appeared to be about eighty, although it's hard to tell what women in their eighties look like as opposed to women in their sixties or seventies. She was tall and muscular, bent slightly in the middle. She looked like someone who was ready to box any creature willing and able to box, at a moment's notice. Instead of a robe, she was wearing a long khaki skirt and a faded yellow button-up blouse.

Her face wasn't so much pearly as weathered and kind of wrinkly, like an apple that's been left out on a window-sill after someone forgot to finish it. She did have very long, flowing white hair down past her knees and, like the

Cloudies, a very long, wispy, wavy beard, which she wore wrapped around her neck like a thick woolen scarf.

The woman thumped over and leaned in close to Ripley with a menacing scowl. "The Cloudies said you're Lumberjanes."

"Yes!" Ripley beamed, moving her face until it was so close to the old woman's face you could barely fit a cat's tail between them. "We're members of Roanoke cabin! Which is the best cabin ever!"

"Humph," the woman said, turning to look April up and down like a sergeant conducting inspection. "If you're LUMBERJANES, why are you out of uniform? Don't tell me they let you wear PANTS." She looked at Jo. "That's not even regulation khaki."

Jo looked down at her pants, which were her favorite pants because they had lots of really big pockets and even two handy secret pockets. "We don't wear uniforms. Lumberjane scouts can wear whatever they want."

"Even tutus," Ripley chimed in. "Or wet suits. Or giant bear costumes! Or clown noses! Or glitter wigs with wings on them. OH! OR—"

"What's that," the old woman pointed a bony finger at Bubbles, who was currently curled up tightly around Jo's neck, while Molly comforted Mal.

"That's our raccoon, Bubbles!" Ripley said. "Technically, it's kind of Molly's raccoon, but now Jo is holding him because there was this fall and—"

"You don't wear uniforms and you carry vermin around?" The old woman snarled, cutting Ripley off. "In my day, a Lumberjane didn't have pets, she had priorities."

"We have both," Jo said, giving Bubbles a reassuring pat on the head.

Bubbles chirped a chirp that might be described as a raccoon saying, "Who is this cantakerous lady, what's her beef with raccoons?!"

April's eyes suddenly popped out of her head. She pointed at the old woman who was giving them static about their clothes. "WHAT THE AGATHA CHRISTIE! YOU'RE a Lumberjane!"

"Humph. Obviously I am," the old woman said, pointing at her uniform, which was faded but clearly Lumberjane green and yellow. "Two points to you for observation skills."

"Hold up," April put her hands on her hips. "You're giving me points?"

"Points are everything to a Lumberjane," the old lady huffed. "I had 4,234 points at last count. And forty-five badges. And a bronze and silver double-ax pin. And the Starbringer medal for fastest runner."

For a brief moment, April wondered how many points she would have, if they gave points. Also she wondered if she should let this woman know how many badges SHE had. Then she shook the thought out of her head.

"I'm sorry." Jo stepped forward. "We didn't introduce ourselves (not that you asked). I'm Jo. This is April, and the person hugging you is Ripley. Over there are our friends Mal and Molly."

"Fine, fine," the woman snapped. Looking down, she added, "No unnecessary displays of affection."

Ripley stepped back. "Sorry. Habit."

"And you are..." Jo asked.

The woman spryly hopped up on a small mound of cloud, waving her finger in the air. "I AM THE LADY DANA DEVEROE ANASTASIA MISTYTOE AND I AM THE GREATEST RECORD HOLDER IN THE HISTORY OF THE LUMBERJANES!"

Pausing for effect, Lady Dana held her hand up in a somewhat majestic gesture.

"You have a record," Jo mused quietly to herself. "Not surprising."

"A record?" Lady Dana cackled. "HA! I have THE RECORDS. All of them! The fastest swim, the longest swim, the fastest unicycle, the fastest climb, and the tallest climb in all of Lumberjane history."

She jumped down and did a few quick laps around April, Jo, and Ripley. "I was the first and, up until you scouts, the only person to climb this mountain."

"This lady is making me dizzy," Ripley said.

"WHAAAA. Wait! You climbed up," April gasped. "And you're STILL here?"

Lady Dana stopped her hopping and finger waving. "HUMPH. You don't know the half of it," she grumbled.

CHAPTER 35

Mal was freaking out. It was embarrassing and frustrating to be the only one in your cabin freaking out. Again. The only one freaked out by being on an alien-looking cloud world with pearl-faced people and no way of getting home.

Or at least the only one who seemed freaked out.

And injured.

So Mal took a moment to stand on a cloud and look at the sky and try to stop from losing her stuffing.

Molly walked up behind Mal and waited for her breathing to get less crazy. Sometimes when Mal got nervous, she kind of hyperventilated a bit. Mal closed her eyes and tried to just breathe.

It took a few minutes. Then Mal took a deep deep breath and let it out.

FFFFFFFFFFFF.

"Hey." Molly's voice was soft and cautious. "I'm sorry about your wrist, Mal. I promise we'll figure out something. There's got to be some way to get down." Molly paused. "And you can go to your accordion practice when it heals."

Mal turned, cheeks red. "I don't care about the accordion. That's not the reason . . . That's not—"

"It's fine," Molly interrupted, suddenly nervous. "I get it. Zodiac are totally cool."

"What?" Mal stepped forward and took Molly's hand with her good hand. "I think *you're* the coolest!"

Molly rolled her eyes, a pinkish color filling her usually pale white cheeks. "I'm not cool."

"You really are," Mal said, running her fingers over the shaved bits of her head nervously. "I'm the one who's not cool. I mean, everything we do as Lumberjanes, I'm always the only one who's freaked out or scared. I'm the only one who's not like, 'Woo-hoo, let's go canoe down a waterfall.'"

"You don't think I was scared when I was falling?" Molly gasped. "I was totally scared!"

"Okay, well." Mal touched her forehead to Molly's forehead. "I'm glad you didn't totally plummet. And I'm glad that even if I'm freaked out, at least you're here."

Suddenly there was an extra pair of arms around them. It was Ripley squeezing them tight.

"April's talking to this grumpy bearded lady who used to be a Lumberjane," she reported in a reporter's voice. "That lady is THE Lady Dana Devotion Alaska Mistletoe . . . or something. She doesn't like hugs and she holds a lot of records and stuff."

"We'll be right there." Molly put her hand on Ripley's head.

"We could all waddle over in hug formation," Ripley suggested, because it sounded like a pretty great idea.

"Okay," Mal said, "but watch my arm."

So the three of them all hug-shuffled back across the clouds to where Lady Dana Deveroe Anastasia Mistytoe was just getting started.

CHAPTER 36

Jo and April watched Lady Dana pace back and forth and back and forth, pinging off an invisible wall, gesturing like she was in a big meeting and trying to make a really big point.

Lady Dana was on her second wind. Maybe even her third. She held her hand up above her head as she continued detailing her string of accomplishments. "I ran through the fields of alabaster wheat and across the Egyptian desert. I swam the Lake of Ruinous Ruin three times around in less time than it took most ladies to get their swimming costumes on. I swam so fast you couldn't even see me swim. I was a BLUR."

"Ruinous Ruin," Mal shivered, as she, Molly, and Ripley approached.

"Swimming costumes," Molly mused.

"There wasn't a race I couldn't win. I was the fastest lap in the 100-, 200- and 2,000-meter sprint," Lady Dana continued, now jogging from foot to foot. "Scouts would say that Lady Dana Deveroe Anastasia Mistytoe is the fastest scout on earth."

"Wow," said April.

"And they were RIGHT!" Lady Dana slammed her fist into her open palm. BOOM!

"I like a snack after a race," Ripley said.

"Being the best runs in my family. My aunt, the great Madam Deborah Darcy Abalonious Mistytoe, rest her soul, used to invent NEW things to be the best at because she ran out." Lady Dana unfurled her long beard from around her neck, tossing it over her shoulder the way old-timey fighter pilots tossed their silk scarves over theirs when they boarded their biplanes

Ripley wondered if it would be rude to ask a person who doesn't like hugging how long it took her to grow her beard. Ripley thought if she herself had a beard, she would dye it different colors like a unicorn tail.

"The Cloudies seem nice," Jo suggested, curious to change the subject from just being really fast.

"They're flakes," Lady Dana muttered, annoyed.

"They don't like to run because they don't want to ruffle their robes."

Gesturing at the mass of clouds, Lady Dana fretted, "Plus since things are always changing around here, no one can be bothered to keep track of anything. So there's no records up here! No fastest times! No points! Just tea and 'weather talk.'"

Lady Dana wrapped her beard back around her neck. "You're going to have to get used to that. You are stuck here now, like me."

April threw her hands up, exasperated. "How can it be there's no way to climb down? When the mountain is THERE, we can just GO."

Lady Dana shook her head. "You don't think I've tried? There's NO path. Unless you have some sort of magical flying machine, you're stuck here."

"Flying machine . . . You mean a plane?" Molly offered, wondering if Lady Dana was so old she didn't know what a plane was.

Lady Dana either didn't hear or was grumpily ignoring Molly.

Mal wondered how it was that someone who was so old she didn't know what a plane was could pace around with that much energy.

Ripley scratched her chin.

Jo wondered how long it would take to rig up a plane. Probably a while.

April was looking at her friends and wondering what the heck her stupid idea had gotten them into this time. Maybe something they would NEVER get out of.

"Humph," Lady Dana said, scratching her beard. "It's time for tea, again. COME ON. You might as well see what the rest of your lives will be like."

CHAPTER 37

The Lumberjanes followed Lady Dana through and over a series of cloudy hills of pink and gray and white and varying degrees of puffy and lumpy and bumpiness.

As April tried to keep up with Lady D, she noticed that in some places the cloud seemed to be coming apart, leaving swirls of curly wisps of cloud floating in the air, like cotton candy in a cotton candy machine.

Eventually, they passed through a cloudy archway and through to what felt like a crater in the cloudy ground, a crater filled with the pearl-faced Cloudies.

The Cloudies, now that it was possible to see a bunch of them, all had pearly faces and beards, they all wore robes, and many of them wore hats. One was wearing what looked like a bowler hat, and one had what looked like a top hat. One had a hat that looked like a pom-pom, and one had a hat that looked a little like a squirrel. All the hats were gray. All the hats seemed to be too small. But also pretty stylish.

"Hey! Dudes! Sunny!" Flap waved lazily from the crowd of Cloudies. "Look, it's the Lumberjanes!"

"Hey, little dudes," Swish said, raising a cup in a toast.

"Humph." Clearly, Lady Dana wasn't feeling sunny.

"Hey, sunny to you too!" Ripley waved back.

"I hope you dudes like tea," Flap said, as another Cloudie appeared, carrying a tray of tiny teacups filled with bubbling cloudy water.

"We do," Jo said, cautiously. "That's very sunny of you to share with us."

Flap nodded vigorously. "Tea is, like, the sunniest thing we have in Cumulous!"

Lady D swiped her cup off the tray and huffed over to a less populated curve of the crater to sip and, seemingly, sulk.

"So what do we do now?" Jo asked the Cloudies, taking a cup from the tray.

"Dudes! Talk about the weather, of course!" Swish sang out brightly.

"Dude," Flap said, "we really love talking about the weather. I hope that's sunny with you."

Another Cloudie in a tiny ten-gallon hat appeared with a tiny teacup. "Yo. It's chillier today than it was yesterday."

"Totally, WHOOSH!" Swish said. "Also it's sunnier."

"Tooootally," Whoosh sipped its tea. "And yesterday, for a moment, I heard rain."

"Dude! I heard the rain too. And last week there was thunder!"

"Interesting," Jo said, taking a sip of tea. "Did you know that the closer together you see lightning and hear thunder, the closer a storm is to where you are? I mean you probably already kn—"

"WHAT?" Whoosh almost dropped its tea. "Dude. Are you serious?"

Whoosh called back to the crater full of Cloudies. "Hey, Bang, Boom, Clap, Flop, Thump! Check it out!"

Soon a cluster of curious Cloudies were all bumping and clumping together around Jo.

"Whoa! Where did you learn about lightning?" they wondered.

Jo shrugged. "I just like reading about stuff. Do you have someone who lets you know what the weather will be? Like a weather . . . uh . . . a weathercloudie?"

The Cloudies' mouths dropped open. "A WHAT?"

Boom braided its beard. "What would that Cloudie do?"

Jo shrugged. "You know, uh, they would read all the atmospheric stuff, like the wind velocity and stuff, and tell you what the weather will be."

"That," Thump looked like it was about to faint, "is the most sun-shower thunder lightning thing I have ever heard."

"A Cloudie"—Swoosh mused, in awe—"who knows what the weather WILL be!"

The rest of the Cloudies gathered around. "Tell us more!"

April peered over at Lady D, who was still sipping and stewing. She leaned in to Jo and whispered, "You got this? I'm going to go check on Lady D."

"I'm talking about science to a bunch of strange creatures living in clouds," Jo whispered back out of the corner of her mouth. "I'm TOTALLY good. Wait until I tell them how lightning CAUSES thunder!"

CHAPTER 38

It did not really look like Lady D wanted company, but April made her way over with her tea anyway.

April sat a careful distance from Lady Dana, on the edge of the cloudy crater and the Cloudie tea party. Lady Dana didn't look up. April took a sip from her cup. The Cloudies' tea tasted a bit like snow water. It had that grainy quality of the snow April used to scoop off the tree branches with her mittens, what she used to call "tree marshmallows."

Mitten snow was also tasty.

Lady Dana slurped from her cup and then turned and squinted at April. "I imagine it's quite a shock, meeting THE Lady Dana Deveroe Anastasia Mistytoe."

"Oh! Um," April crossed her feet nervously, "sure . . ."

Lady Dana sipped her tea. "My plaques are still mounted and on display? My records still lauded at all meets and tournaments? Do they still announce the names of past victors before each competition?"

"Um," April looked at her lap, "well, um, not . . ."

Lady Dana put her tea down with a CLANK. "Spit it out, scout."

April shrugged. "I mean, there's lots of different places where scouts put up their records and stuff. There's this place in the mess hall where you can see Ripley's record for the most pancakes eaten . . ."

Lady Dana looked at April. Cold as a handful of ice cubes.

"Heh heh. Quite a mouthful," April smiled.

Lady Dana scowled. Thunder.

"It's a pun, uh, sort of . . ." April said.

"You were completely unaware of my achievements?" Lady Dana fumed.

"Sorry," April said. "I mean, I—"

"Well, isn't that just DANDY!" Lady Dana grumbled, picking up her tea again. "The whole system down the tubes! NO POINTS. NO RECORDS! So it's just a bunch of amateurs running around not caring who is fastest and who can jump the longest or the highest?"

April shook her head. "No! I mean, there are still badges and sometimes there are competitions. We just, I mean we all try to do great things and learn new things, we just . . . I mean, we just got our Living the Plant Life badge, and Barney's going to get . . . a badge, I don't know, I told them to get their sailing badge, but Ripley said they're going to do the Fondant badge instead . . ."

Lady Dana sipped her tea. "I gather you've earned your talking-too-much badge."

April took a sip of her tea. There wasn't a talking-too-much badge, actually. There was a Tip of the Tongue badge for talking fast, which April didn't have . . . yet. April could say something about Lady Dana getting her cantankerous-and-crabby badge but that seemed . . . not a good idea.

"I'm sure you don't know this," Lady Dana turned her face to the sky, "because it seems there is very little you DO know, but before THE Lady Dana Deveroe Anastasia Mistytoe, there WAS no climbing record. I was the first!"

Lady Dana paused, took a sip of tea, and added, in a grumble, "If this had been an actual mountain, I would have also had the record for most peaks discovered. If this WAS an actual mountain."

"Because it's not on a map," April whispered.

"Yes." Lady Dana took a slurp of tea. "It was a great opportunity. An opportunity for greatness."

"But it's not a mountain." April looked across the clouds at her friends all drinking tea with the Cloudies. Molly reached up and touched one of the Cloudies' gray hats.

"No," Lady Dana said.

April looked at her cup.

Lady D looked at April. "I'm assuming you had similar motivations."

"I did it, I mean, we climbed . . . because," April frowned, "because . . . I mean, I don't hold a zillion records, but I'm trying to get all the badges, or a lot of them. I mean, I guess getting badges is kind of something I'm really good at and I love doing. And . . . I wanted to win this medal, the Extraordinary Explorers medal. Rosie, she's our camp director, she has it."

"You wanted to be the best," Lady Dana said.

April frowned. "I didn't want to be the best, I just, I wanted to be the best Lumberjane I could be and . . ."

April's face fell. "And I had this plan, and normally they work, I mean most of the time they work." April's cheeks went red. "But this time it really didn't work. We didn't explore anything. This Mountain doesn't even exist. And Mal's hurt. And my friends are stuck here forever."

"It appears so," Lady Dana said.

"Hey!" A Cloudie wearing a stocking cap almost as long as its beard came by with a giant pot. "More tea? It's super sunny."

April shook her head.

"No, thank you." Lady Dana tucked her mug in her beard.

"Okay then!" The Cloudie wandered off.

April covered her face with her hands.

Lady Dana sniffed, got up, and walked to wherever it is Lumberjanes with beards go after tea.

April felt pretty stormy. Like there was an actual storm brewing on top of her actual head.

A small bolt of lightning flashed in her brain.

April stood up, clenching her fists. "No," she said. "We're not stuck up here. I'm going to find a way down."

And with that, April was up and running—past Jo, who was talking about barometric pressure to the Cloudies; past Ripley, who was trying on a spare Cloudie robe for size; past Mal and Molly, who were putting on little Cloudie hats.

Friendship to the max, you guys, even when it looks glum. Friendship to the max.

CHAPTER 39

April was already knee-deep in the pile of frayed bits of rope when the rest of the Lumberjanes found her.

"Okay. SO! NEW PLAN. We piece together what we have," she said, holding up the frayed ends and talking fast. "We can add our sweaters, socks, whatever fabric we have free, and you guys can lower me down. As close to the ground as we can get. And I'll jump. No problem. I'll go and get someone with a flying machine and—"

Jo shook her head. "Bad plan. We don't know how far it is! We don't have near enough fabric or rope!"

"Good plan!" April insisted. "I could get close!" April wrung her hands, her eyes huge and pleading. "Come on, it's worth a try."

Molly stepped over and took the rope from April's hand. "April. We're not going to let you dangle yourself off a cloud."

"Yeah." Ripley frowned, crossing her arms over her chest. "No dangling. Dangling BAD."

"April," Mal said quietly, cradling her sore arm against her chest, "you don't have to fix this."

April stepped over and took Mal's good hand in hers. "Mal, I'm so sorry. I'm so sorry we did this thing and you got hurt! I didn't think. I just thought about this thing I wanted to do! I didn't think about—"

Mal squeezed April's hand. "WE'RE going to make a new plan. We're going to figure out something out, April. And not something that puts YOU in danger."

Ripley looked down at her hand, and the only slightly wilted Clow Bell she was still holding.

"Hey," she said to April, holding out the tiny flower, "here. It's a Clow Bell from Dr. Twinkle. To make you feel better."

April took the flower carefully. It bobbed in the breeze. "Thanks, Ripley."

"Hey, did we ever find out why they're called Clow Bells?" Molly wondered. "They don't look anything like a bell."

"Oh! It's because they make a little sound," Mal said, pointing to her ear. "Listen."

April watched the bell sway in the gentle breeze. It did make a sound. It wasn't a very big sound; in fact, it was one of the tiniest sounds she had ever heard. It was like the size of a sound you would imagine coming from a ladybug, if ladybugs could talk.

Maybe they can.

Anyway, it was definitely a very small but distinct sound.

A eureka moment is when a person suddenly figures out a solution to a problem, also called an aha moment. This is obviously very different from a ha ha moment.

An image popped into Mal's head. It was of her grandma, the one who played the flute and had three little gray cats that used to play in the backyard and steal laundry from the neighbors' lines. At the end of the day, her grandma used to stand in the doorway of the kitchen, looking out over the garden, and she'd hit a tin of cat food with a fork until the cats bounced in from the backyard.

Mal flashed back to Molly shaking the Clow Bell at the unicorn.

"Hey," she said, her face lighting up with a cool idea.

At the same time, Jo was thinking about the unicorns. About walking behind them, that first day, about how the unicorns didn't leave any hoof (foot, whatever) prints behind. Jo thought about the unicorns whizzing around the fields of Clow Bells.

"Hey," Jo said.

Mal looked at April. "OMG, NEW PLAN," she said.

Jo nodded. "Me too. We need to talk to the Cloudies."

PART FOUR

KEEP IT TOGETHER BADGE

"Don't break the chain."

Working as a team is essential to the success of any Lumberjane endeavor. Lumberjanes know that are a lot of things you can do by yourself, but there are a million more things you can do as a team. These things include volleyball, baseball, basketball, hockey, tennis, cricket, and almost any other sport that isn't golf. These things also include basic things like building a fire, a tent, a canoe, or anything else that requires a little bit of ingenuity.

When you work as a team, you combine the insights and energies of several Lumberjanes. Also, periodically, it will be useful for one Lumberjane to stand on another's shoulders to see over a tall wall or climb a very tall tree.

Of course, in each of these cases, the following precautions should be . . .

CHAPTER 40

When the Lumberjanes got back to the crater, the tea party was still in full swing. The Cloudies were still talking about the weather, possibly even more excitedly than usual.

"If this works, we could talk about even MORE weather," Whoosh gushed.

"SO SUNNY!" Flap cheered.

Boom clapped its hands together excitedly.

Swish braided its beard, which is what Swish did when it was excited. "Hey, look, it's Jo! Yo, Jo, do you want more tea?"

Jo shook her head. "We have a quick question for you."

"Totally," Flap said. "Sup?"

"Have you ever seen a unicorn?" Jo asked. "A horse with a tail, and a horn on its head." Jo looked at the Cloudies, who seemed to be looking blankly back at her. "Oh, do I need to explain 'horse'?"

Swished shook its head. "Nah! We know unicorns! They're those smelly guys! Those dudes are up here all the time, like, zigging and zagging through the clouds and stuff, like little zigzag dudes."

"Wait," April looked at Jo, wide-eyed, "unicorns can fly? How did you know unicorns could fly?"

Jo turned to April. "Remember when we were following the unicorn in the forest and watching them in the fields? They don't leave any hoofprints," Jo explained. "I just had this thought, like, maybe they can fly."

"Also gas," Molly offered.

"Unicorn farts are probably pretty powerful," Ripley added.

"That's supersmart, Jo!" April chucked Jo on the shoulder. "Two points for smart."

"Thanks. I'll take those two points and give you two back for the cool compliment."

"Accepted." April turned to the tea-sipping Cloudies. "Is there any specific place you've seen the unicorns?"

"Oh, uh," Swish scratched its head below its fuzzy cap. "Yeah. Uh. Do you want us to show you?"

"Yes," Mal said emphatically. "That would be totally sunny."

Flap and Swish, and Boom and Whoosh, put their cups down and gestured with their long, lazy hands to all the Lumberjanes to follow.

Past a series of puffy cloud banks shaped like penguins, muffins, and mushrooms, they came to a small gap, a hole the size of a backyard pool in the clouds.

Molly looked down through the clouds. There was the rest of the world. But it was very very very far away. The unicorns weren't even dots anymore, they were blurry pixels indistinguishable from everything else. The wind whistled along the edge of the white bank. "Wow."

"Dudes." Mal whistled.

"Totally, dudes! That's where those unicornies like to pop up," Flap said. "But it's, like, kind of rando."

"Okay," April turned to look at Mal and Jo. "So. Now what?"

"Now we call the cats home!" Mal said, pointing at the Clow Bell in April's hand.

"Cats!" Ripley jumped. "There's cats?! AMAZING!"

"No," Mal said, "but there's unicorns."

"And we call them with the Clow Bells?" Molly tilted her head.

Mal smiled at Molly.

"Remember how Molly got the unicorn to follow us by holding out the Clow Bells," Mal explained. "So. They eat them all the time; they would have become attuned to the sound they make. So maybe if we ring them, maybe they'll come up!"

"Genius," Molly said, carefully taking Mal's good hand.

"Two points for genius," Jo added, pointing at Mal.

"WE HAVE SO MANY POINTS NOW!" Ripley cheered.

April looked at the now slightly more wilted flower. "Do you think this one Clow Bell is enough?"

"I think it would help if we had more," Jo admitted. "But that's what we've got."

"WAIT!" Ripley cheered. Reaching into her backpack, she pulled out her sweatshirt, which was rolled around . . . a whole bunch of . . . Clow Bells!

"RIPLEY!" April gasped. "This is the best bouquet EVER!"

"I thought I would put them in the cabin for later in case we saw more unicorns," Ripley admitted. "But we can use them now."

"Okay." Jo picked up the flowers and passed them around to the other scouts. "Let's do this, Lumberjanes."

"And Cloudies," Ripley said. "Cloudies can help!"

And so everyone, including Flap, Swish, Boom, and

Whoosh, stood by the edge of the cloud, holding a delicate flower in each hand.

Almost everyone.

"HEY!" Lady Dana arrived with her beard flowing out behind her. "What are you doing now?"

"RINGING UP SOME UNICORNS," April said. "Want to join us?"

"Humph," Lady Dana said, folding her arms over her chest.

"Okay," Jo said. "Everyone else ready?"

"Yes!"

"YAS!"

"Let's do it!"

"Yes!!"

"Ya, dudes."

"Totally."

CHAPTER 41

Rosie!" Jen pointed. "LOOK!"

The unicorns froze. All at once. Like someone had pressed pause on the unicorn movie.

They pricked up their ears.

And listened.

"Hmmm," said Rosie.

One unicorn in particular, with a purple and gold tail, raised its head up high. It shook its head. It whinnied. Like you would whinny if you were calling out, "COMING!"

Then, all at once, the unicorns shifted, like a wind picking up and blowing across the fields. They started to buck and rear up. Then they started to run.

"This could be something," Rosie said, grabbing Jen's hand. "Let's go."

"Go?" Jen twisted to follow Rosie. "Go where?"

The unicorns began to run in a circle, gathering up in a wave, a wave that was gaining momentum and lifting off the ground.

"I think it's going to be UP," Rosie said, and the two of them started to run. "Get ready to ride, Jet!"

"It's JEN! And, uh, while we're on the subject, have you ever ridden a unicorn before?" Jen hollered as they closed in on the cyclone of zipping unicorns.

"NO!" Rosie hollered back. "It's going to be FUN!"

The unicorns were kicking up their own gale-force wind tunnel.

A wind tunnel that smelled like a very old dog blanket soufflé.

Rosie and Jen plunged forward into the twister of tails and horns.

Having taken half a second to think it over, Rosie offered this insight: "I'm thinking it's going to be a little like riding a Ferrantio," she shouted, as she reached out for a flying mane. "Minus the wings and hopefully minus the biting."

"MINUS THE WHAT!?"

"HANG ON!"

CHAPTER 42

At first, there was not much to see, just a bunch of Lumberjanes and a few Cloudies waving flowers in the air next to a hole in the cloud.

Not that that itself wasn't interesting, it just wasn't very rescue-y.

April waved her flowers with her eyes closed. Hoping. Hoping. Hoping.

"Is this what they teach you at Lumberjanes?" Lady Dana fumed, pacing behind them. "Flower waving? Minus two points for weird ideas."

"Lumberjanes love weird ideas!" Molly called behind her. "Plus a million points for weird ideas!"

"Heck ya," Ripley said, pleased that they were still on a good point streak.

"Truth," Jo nodded.

April frowned. This had to work. Had to. Had to.

"Just wait," Mal said.

"Wait for WHAT?" Lady Dana barked.

"Sometimes it takes a while for something to work," Molly said, patiently.

"They're coming!" Ripley sang out. "I can smell them! They're coming!"

"Yeek," Mal said, but still, it was not the worst thing in the world. Because yes, it smelled awful, a wave of old eggs in a bed of Ferrantio droppings, but here they came!

A cacophony of unicorns, with pink tails and blue tails and green tails and red tails all aflutter, sparkling in the sun and smelling not unlike a rising tide of very old tuna fish sandwiches (if old tuna fish sandwiches could fly), emerged from the clouds. It was like a parade of unicorns, but slightly more chaotic. Somewhere in the bustle of bright colors, Rosie and Jen waved ecstatically.

"WOOO-HOOO!" Rosie called. "The cavalry has arrived!"

"GIRLS!" Jen cried, holding on to her unicorn with both arms. "YOU'RE ALIVE!"

"JEN!" Mal and Molly cried.

"ROSIE!" April jumped up and down.

HOORAY!

"UNICOOOOORNS!" Ripley trilled, whirling in the air, shaking her Clow Bells. "THIS IS AMAZING!"

It's worth pointing out, for anyone who has plans to RIDE a unicorn, that there is no real command to get a unicorn to stop. Additionally, as noted earlier, unicorns don't really like to take a direct route anywhere, so it took a little bit of time for the rave of unicorns to actually land on the cloudy crest.

The unicorn Jen was riding opted to take a few extra loops through the clouds before coming to a screeching halt that kicked up a significant amount of cloud.

Ripley recognized him immediately. "DR. TWINKLE!" she cried, adding, "JEN!"

As soon as she was sure they weren't about to take another loop, Jen projectile-dismounted off her unicorn and was immediately pounced on by April, Ripley, Jo, Mal, and Molly. "YOU GUYS, I WAS SO WORRIED!" Jen gasped from under a pile of grateful scouts, eyes wide. "Are you okay?"

"Um," Jo said, "not really, actually."

"WHAT?"

Mal held out her arm. "I might have sprained my wrist during our death-defying ascent."

"YOU HAD A DEATH-DEFYING ACCENT?"

"Ascent." Molly clarified. "Although it would be cool to have a death-defying accent."

"Actually, it was on a descent that this happened," Mal said, pointing downward.

Jen pressed her hands against her cheeks, her eyes full of worry. "MAL!"

Rosie, whose unicorn was now munching on the Clow Bell that April dropped, leaned in and took a closer look. "Could be a sprain," she said. "We need to get you to first aid. Ice will bring down the swelling."

"We should get going," Jen said, taking Mal's good hand in hers. "Who knows how long it will take these nutty unicorns to get us back to camp."

"Wait," April looked around. "What happened to Lady Dana Deveroe Anastasia Mistytoe?"

CHAPTER 43

Jo and April spotted the lady in question walking away from the crowd of unicorns and scouts. Her beard wavered in the breeze as she strode off, huffing and humphing.

April ran up next to her and threw her hands in the air. "Hey, we're rescued!" She cheered. "We can go home!"

"Humph!" Lady Dana Deveroe Anastasia Mistytoe's lips curled. "Quite the rescue. A bunch of nincompoop unicorns smelling like yesterday's whoopee cushions. Don't let the cloud bank hit you on the derriere on your way out."

"Wait," Jo said, confused, "you know what a whoopee cushion is but you don't know what a plane is?"

Lady Dana didn't seem to hear Jo. She slowed a bit. Then stopped. Then she turned to April and Jo, her face twisted into a scowl. "The sooner you rabble-rousers get off of Cumulous, the better. So make it snappy."

April pressed her hands together at her chest. "But. Don't you want to come with us? Back to camp?"

"Yeah," Jo nodded, "once a Lumberjane always a Lumberjane!"

Lady Dana shook her head. "No, thank you. I am perfectly content."

April looked at Jo. Jo looked at April and shrugged.

"We can't just leave her here," April whispered.

"But she doesn't want to leave," Jo whispered back.

"Two points off for rudeness!" Lady Dana barked. "I'm old, not deaf. I said I don't want to leave and I meant it."

April twisted her lips to the left and the right. "I don't understand."

"Well then, you're not very smart, are you?" Lady Dana frowned.

"Actually," Jo frowned back, "April is very very smart."

Lady Dana pulled on her beard. "Call me an old lady set in her ways—"

"Okay," Jo said. "You're an old lady set in your ways."

"That may be. But I'm still THE Lady Dana Deveroe Anastasia Mistytoe, and I like what I like. From what you say, the Lumberjanes aren't what they used to be. And if it's not the way it was, I'd rather stay here and have tea with the dim-witted Cloudies. At least here my records stand."

"Life is more than records," April said. "It's more than great accomplishments and mountains."

"Humph. Well, that's what you think," Lady Dana retorted.

April looked down at the Clow Bell in her hand. "Okay," she said, "but I'm leaving you with this." She placed the wilted Clow Bell in Lady Dana's hand. "If you ever want to come down, you should just ring this, okay?"

Lady Dana looked at the Clow Bell. She twisted her beard tighter around her neck. "Seems unlikely," she said. "But two points for helping out an old lady, I guess. Now, go on, scram."

"Well," April said, "I'm glad I got to meet you, THE Lady Dana Deveroe Anastasia Mistytoe. I'm always going to remember you."

And with that, Lady Dana turned on her heels and strode off into the increasingly violet sky.

"Hey," Jo put a hand on April's shoulder. "The unicorns await."

The unicorns were getting restless. There were no more Clow Bells to munch on and it was time to get zigzagging. Rosie and Ripley got on Dr. Twinkle. Mal and Molly got a tight grip on a relatively docile unicorn with a long, flowing mane the color of emeralds. Jo and April doubled on a chubby little unicorn with a sky-blue tail and a curly mane the color of blueberry pie. Jen clutched the neck of a prancing unicorn with a feathery golden tail, and Bubbles clutched onto Jen with equal vigor.

It was time to go. Dr. Twinkle let out a whinny like, "COME ON, ALREADY!"

The Cloudies paused to wave good-bye before going back to tea. "Bye! Don't come back! 'Cause it's totally super thunder and lightning climbing up here, and you need to stay where it's sunny. Okay?"

"Okay!" Ripley waved enthusiastically. "Bye, Cloudies!"

Rosie nodded a quick good-bye, let out a shrill whistle, and they were off.

The unicorns rose up, soaring over the expanse of pinkish cloud, and whirled up high into the sky in a spiral of unicorns, then zipped down, plunging through the hole in the cloud like a bolt of lightning headed earthward.

"I've got you," Molly whispered, wrapping her arms tight around Mal's waist, the wind whipping through their hair.

As her unicorn zigged, April looked up and scanned the horizon of cloud for Lady Dana. But she was nowhere in sight.

"FAREWELL, LADY DANA!" April called anyway, as her unicorn swept past the cloudy world on top of the mountain that wasn't a mountain.

It was possible that, wherever she was, Lady Dana said good-bye too.

CHAPTER 44

Flying on a unicorn, for all its zigs and zags, is a pretty divine experience. Highly recommended if you find a unicorn willing to give you a ride.

After a bit of a shaky start, a few turns that seemed a little sharper than necessary, the unicorns settled into an easy flow, banking left and right, soaring over treetops, dipping their hooves into the lake as they glided over the broken reflection of the setting sun on the water's surface. Over the sound of happy unicorn neighs, Ripley's giggles of joy could be heard, which made even Rosie smile a little.

Mal was freaked but she tried to focus on what she could see in front of her instead of looking down at the ground whizzing by like the world was on fast-forward.

Molly did her best to help Mal stay steady, given she could hold on with only one hand.

The wind whipped Molly's hair into her face and she closed her eyes. How amazing was it to go to a camp that involved, sometimes, flying?

Jo marveled at the relatively strange aerodynamics at play in the unicorns' flight. Which is what you tend to marvel at when your gay dads spend most of their breakfasts talking about drag, when drag is a force that acts in the opposite direction of a moving force—and also the subject of their favorite TV show.

April was thinking about Lady Dana, up in the clouds, grouchily resting on her laurels and sipping tea with the Cloudies.

Fortunately for everybody, the unicorns seemed to sense they were carrying injured passengers on this second pass, and they came to a gentle stop in the fields of Clow Bells. They even waited for the Lumberjanes to dismount before they recommenced zipping around and munching in the fields that served as their happy home.

The sun was setting. The sky was turning eye shadow purple and pink and yellow.

Jeremy the moose, who had been wondering where everyone went, was there to carry Mal and Rosie back to camp.

"I'll see you guys in a bit!" Mal waved from Jeremy's back.

"Come on, Jeremy," Rosie urged, making a series of tick-ticking noises. It was nice to be riding something that smelled just like moose, she thought, which is not an unpleasant smell when you're used to it.

"Right," Jen said, turning to the rest of the scouts. "NO messing around. We're going RIGHT back to camp."

"YA!" Ripley said, as she turned and did a jumping wave at the unicorns. "GOOD-BYE, DR. TWINKLE!"

"Holy Julia Child, I'm starving," Molly said, grabbing her stomach as they marched after Jen.

"Maybe there's some leftover chili," Jo offered, with a sly grin.

"Yeek," Molly said, "I don't know if my stomach is up for a near-death experience, a unicorn flight, AND more chili."

"YAY CHILI!" Ripley cheered, doing her own version of a zigzag home, with Bubbles in hot pursuit.

April stopped, for just a second. How could something like a medal or a mountain be so important one minute, so important it filled your whole body, and the next minute not even there, not important at all? At her feet were the puzzled-out pieces of the sign. The warning they missed. Beyond that, no mountain. Just the horizon and the setting sun.

Molly reached back and grabbed April's arm. "Come on," she said, "I bet someone's set up the bonfire. Let's go."

And so Jo and Ripley and April and Molly and Jen headed back into the woods. And the unicorns were left to chomp peacefully in the shadow of a mountain that wasn't there.

CHAPTER 45

There is little in this world that is more magical than a bonfire.

It was Zodiac's turn to start the fire, which Barney lit with a bow drill, which is a contraption, consisting of a spindle and a piece of wood, that lets you light a fire using friction. Which means you have to use a sawing motion, and a tool that looks like a bow, to spin the spindle until you get a spark.

It didn't take long for the spark to become a flame and, with a little coaxing from some moss and kindling that Woolpit cabin gathered from the woods that day, a fire.

When the fire was roaring, scouts gathered from all the cabins. The Zodiac scouts hauled over their accordions and someone from Roswell brought a guitar. Maddy, from Woolpit, had a tambourine.

"So," Wren from Zodiac asked, "what are we singing?"

Mal came back from the first aid tent with an ice pack on her arm and sat next to Molly on one of the logs next to the fire. "Nurse Carol says she thinks it's just bruised," she said happily. "So I should be okay in a day or so."

"That's awesome," Molly said, wrapping her arm around Mal's shoulder.

The Zodiac scouts were trying their hand at an accordion version of "My Bonnie Lies over the Ocean."

"Bleh," Mal said, sticking her tongue out. "If we're going to play with Zodiac, we're going to have to pick some better music."

"*We're* going to play?" Molly raised an eyebrow and pointed at herself doubtfully.

"Well, yeah," Mal said. "I mean, if we do it together, does that sound like something you'd want to do?"

Molly looked over at Zodiac. Zodiac looked like they were having fun. Wren had her hair tied up on the top of her head, and she was kicking left and right as she pulled the folds of the accordion open and closed. She shut her eyes when she played. The light from the fire reflected off the keys as her fingers danced up and down.

"I might suck," Molly said, looking at her feet.

"There's no way you're going to suck," Mal said, taking Molly's hand with her good hand. "And it will be cool to learn something together! We can be the left hand and the right hand!"

Molly nodded. "Okay. Okay, we'll learn the accordion. Together."

"Excellent." Mal looked into the flames, a small smile on her face.

"I'm going to get us some s'more stuff," Molly said. And she gave Mal a small kiss on her forehead before heading off looking for marshmallows. "Thanks for asking me to play music with you."

Zodiac switched from "My Bonnie Lies over the Ocean" to The Supremes' "You Keep Me Hangin' On," which is slightly harder to play but, Mal thought, a way cooler song.

CHAPTER 46

By the time April had taken her seat on a log next to the fire pit, the flames were greedily dancing on the big logs, reaching up into the sky with little flame fingers.

Jo helped Ripley rig up a multi-toasting-stick configuration so she could roast five marshmallows at a time.

April put her chin in her hands, feeling the heat on her face, the cold night air on her back.

After she was sure Ripley wasn't going to burn everything to a crisp, Jo came back and plopped down next to April on her log. "Hey," April murmured.

"Hey," Jo said. "You okay?"

"I'm just in my brain replaying the worst plan in all of Lumberjane history," April said, not looking up, "which almost got some of the most important people in my world squished or stranded on top of a cloud. Rosie even told us . . . BE PREPARED . . . KNOW as much as possible before heading out on an adventure, and I didn't do any of that."

Jo patted April on the back. "Yeah, okay, but it's also because of you we ended up saved, right? Because of your wicked lasso skills? If it wasn't for your quick thinking, we'd be pancakes."

Mal and Molly arrived with more snacks and plopped down next to April on her log. "Hey, what's going on?" Mal asked.

"I'm apologizing for almost getting all of you squished and getting your arm hurt," April said.

Mal grabbed April in a hug with her good arm. "It's okay. Look, the nurse said my wrist is just a little bruised. I'm going to be fine."

"You didn't know it wasn't going to be a mountain long enough for us to climb all the way up and all the way down," Molly said, jumping up to give April a squeeze.

"I would have if I'd read the signs," April grumbled. "If I'd looked up . . . the weather."

"Well, none of us read the signs," Jo said. "I mean, we didn't see the signs, but we should have looked. So we all blew it on that one. You know what else?"

"What?"

Just then, Ripley bounced over, her hands full to bursting with toasted marshmallows. Bubbles bounced in with paws full of marshmallow roasting sticks. "HEY!! Hey, what's going on?"

"We're talking with April about the most important part of being a Lumberjane," Mal said. "Which is what?"

Ripley jumped up in a perfect starfish formation, tossing the marshmallows in the air. "FRIENDSHIP TO THE MAX!!!"

"That's exactly right." Jo stood and started gathering the marshmallows. "Even if things went wrong, even if we made some bad decisions, we were still totally FRIENDSHIP TO THE MAX, and that's what being a Lumberjane is all about!"

"Hey," Mal said, "if it wasn't for FRIENDSHIP, we'd all still be up in the clouds with Old Cranky Pants Swimming Costume and her band of Cloudies. We all worked together in perfect harmony in the end, right?"

"When we work TOGETHER," Molly said, "WE come up with awesome plans."

"Let's never stop making plans," Ripley sighed. "I love our adventures."

April smiled a little smile. "Group hug formation?"

"YES!"

"GENIUS!"

"TWO POINTS FOR GENIUS!"

"HOORAY!"

On the other side of the campfire, the makeshift band of accordions and tambourines and the Lumberjane choir broke into a Lumberjane favorite, Sleater-Kinney's "Get Up."

It's not the official Lumberjanes camp song, but it's a good song for a campfire and group hugs.

CHAPTER 47

The fire shifted into glowing ember mode and the stars twinkled (which is stars' main mode). Campers full of s'mores and other fireside snacks drifted back to their cabins until only Roanoke remained.

April munched her fourth and possibly final marshmallow of the night.

"So Lady Dana was the most record-holding Lumberjane in the history of all time," Mal said. "When was she even a camper?"

"I don't know," April said. "When there were swimming costumes and whoopee cushions."

"She might not be the record holder anymore." Jo picked a little bit of marshmallow off her finger. "I think a lot of Lumberjanes are the types of people who do a lot of stuff. Plus the thing about records is they're kind of made to be broken. Also, DUDE!" Jo shook her hand violently. "Cooked marshmallow is like GLUE."

"Cloudy," April said.

"My pancakes record will never be broken," Ripley grinned. "MY RECORD IS UNBREAKABLE!"

"Yes, because the human stomach has its limits," Jo agreed.

"Mmmmmm." Molly was also trying to get the marshmallow off her fingers, using the log as a wooden dish towel. "I will say, records or not, for a Lumberjane, Lady Dana was not Friendship to the Max."

"Yeah," Mal said. "Also BTW, the archway out front says HARDCORE LADY TYPES. It doesn't say, MOST BADGES EVER, FASTEST RUNNER."

"Good point." April wondered if there was a pun in there. She was just about to take a stab at it when—

"Evening, campers," Rosie hooted, arriving with an armful of wood. "That was quite a day! My first unicorn ride!"

Dropping her hefty pile next to the fire, Rosie wiped her forehead with her bandanna.

April raised her hand.

"Yes, April."

"Um. Hey. Question. Did you ever end up like that, um, ever?" April asked Rosie. "I mean, stuck, like that."

Rosie cracked her back and stretched. "Like any good explorer, I have been lost many times."

Ripley looked over from her roasting spot. "Does one of the times have a really good story?"

"Yes," Rosie said, taking a seat next to Jo on the log.

CAMPFIRE STORY TIME!

FINALLY!

"It was in my earlier scouting days," Rosie said, leaning back, the flames reflecting in her glasses. "Goddess, this was so many years ago. My friend Abigail and I heard these other scouts at lunch, talking about a certain raging water dragon."

"Raging water dragon?" April said, her ears pricking up.

"Yes." Rosie raised an eyebrow. "Linus. A particularly ornery raging water dragon."

April was practically leaning over Jo's lap, her eyes like saucers. "Ornery? Please continue!"

Rosie shifted on the log. "We headed out, Abi and I; we had a raft and some rope and a giant jar of jelly beans. So we were prepared."

"Jelly beans?" Mal asked.

"For Linus," Rosie said, like everyone knows that, which maybe they do.

"JELLY BEANS," Ripley waved her arms ecstatically, then added in a hushed voice, "Rosie is telling a story."

Rosie continued. "We got to where the waterfalls were supposed to be; that was a good long hike. Way longer than I expected. Also we ran into a colossal herd of transfixed turtles on the way, transfixed SNAPPING turtles, and that was a whole heap of to do, as you can imagine."

Everyone nodded.

"So there we are lugging around this huge jar of jelly beans and it's getting dark, and there's a hole in my bag, and the jelly beans have leaked out, and it's getting cold, when I realize . . ." Rosie chuckled, slapping her knee. "We'd been using the wrong map!"

"Whoa," April breathed. "WHAAA?"

"So we were nowhere near Linus AND we were lost. Holy cats, we were lost. Abigail was pretty steamed." Rosie grinned wickedly. "Fortunately, because we'd been spilling jelly beans the whole way we were able to Hansel and Gretel our way back to camp."

"Lucky," Molly breathed.

"Did you go back to find Linus?" April asked. "Is that how you got your Extraordinary Explorers medal?

Rosie shrugged. "You know, I don't know when we got that medal. After a few badges, it all kind of blurs together. Mostly I remember the adventures, not accolades. Medals are just medals. It's not like they're going to help you over a cliff or find you drinking water in the desert."

"True," April said.

Rosie looked at April and snapped her fingers. "Almost forgot."

Reaching into her back pocket, she pulled out April's notebook and handed it to her. "I believe this is yours."

"Hey! I didn't even know I dropped it! Thanks!" April hugged the book to her chest.

"All right then." Rosie stepped away from the fire. "Good night, scouts."

Jo looked at April's notebook. "You know," she said, "the thing that's amazing about you, the thing we all think is so great, isn't just the amazing things you do, or your badges or any of that, it's how much you love all this stuff."

April tucked her notebook under her arm. It felt good to have it back. "Yeah?"

"YEAH!" The other members of Roanoke cried out in chorus.

"Well, I love you guys the most," April said.

"YEFF!" Ripley agreed, her mouth full of marshmallow.

Jo looked up at the sky. "Also . . ."

"ALSO!" April squealed, jumping up. "THERE'S A WATER DRAGON NAMED LINUS!"

"Right," Mal said, "but before we go looking for him,

I'm going to crash and sleep the sleep of a thousand Mals."

"Good idea," Molly added.

"I guess we don't want the night to DRAG-ON!" April grinned.

Jen arrived just in time to help carry Ripley, who was totally sugar-crashing, back to Roanoke for a well-deserved rest.

CHAPTER 48

"Get some sleep," Jen advised, as she stood in the doorway with her hand on the light switch. "You guys have a ton of stuff to do tomorrow, since you did nothing from my carefully prepared list."

Mal, Molly, and Ripley were dreaming the moment their heads hit their pillows. Bubbles, who was curled up in a bunch of laundry on the floor, was snoring the loudest.

April sat on her bed with flashlight in hand, her notebook in her lap.

Next to the drawing of the mountain she wrote, "This is not a mountain." Also, "Last known sighting of the great Lady Dana Deveroe Anastasia Mistytoe."

Then she flipped the page over and wrote, "LINUS THE WATER DRAGON????"

Then she closed her book.

First, sleep.

There are a lot of places an adventure—and lessons—can go, once you're done with them. Into a notebook is one place. Or a book of any kind is handy, because that way you can always remember it.

This time, as April lay in bed, the adventure seemed to be settling somewhere else as well.

April put her hands over her heart.

She reached her toe up and poked Jo's bunk.

"Good night," she whispered.

"Night," Jo whispered back.

Jo had already clicked off her flashlight. She was looking out her window, at the big moon shining so brightly she didn't even need a flashlight.

Of course, Jo knew how far away the moon was from Earth. Still it was interesting to note how close it seemed tonight. Like Jo could almost reach out and touch—

Jo leaned forward and pressed her hands against the glass of her window.

Was it closer tonight? It was. But that's impossible, Jo thought.

But it was closer. In fact, the trees shuddered as something that looked very much like the moon settled closer still, pushing down through their branches like a giant ship parting the waves. Jo closed her eyes. Was she dreaming? Can you close your eyes in a dream? There was a shudder, a small earth shake. When she opened her eyes again, the moon . . . was there, maybe twenty feet away, glowing.

And something, or someone, stepped off its cratered surface, into the dark of night.

SOME LUMBERJANES BADGES!

ABSENCE MAKES THE HEART GROW FONDANT

Cake decorating is the art of creating flora and fauna in sugar form. Yum!

GET ON UP!

Get ready, mountaineers! It's time to reach new heights! With this badge, Lumberjanes learn the basics of knots, ropes, and gravity to surmount the mountain face.

GOURMET IT OVER WITH

Fine dining is for everyone! Lumberjanes take on the basics of the three-, seven-, twelve-, and twenty-course feast, including everything from charcuterie to aperitifs!

FIRST THINGS FIRST AID

Tourniquets, larger bandages, splints, and Band-Aids. Learn how to apply a little possibly lifesaving care to your fellow scouts!

I SAW THE SIGNS
Reading is knowledge and knowledge is power. Learn to read the signs marking your path and make sure you're on the right one!

KEBAB'S YOUR UNCLE
Meat on a stick. This badge covers everything from spices to the fine art of grilling.

KEEP IT TOGETHER
Lumberjanes stick together! What else do you need to know?!

LIVING THE PLANT LIFE
Learn the basics of what's green and grows in the amazing natural world.

MAY THE FORGE BE WITH YOU
Harness the power of fire to manipulate metal! With this badge, Lumberjanes discover the joys of metalsmithing.

MY FAIR LASSO
Rope 'em up with this possibly lifesaving skill. All you need is a rope and a lot of time to practice getting that rope around another object.

PEACE AND QUILT

Every quilt tells the story of a bunch of pieces of fabric carefully stitched together. Plus quilts keep you warm!

S'MORE THE MERRIER

Become the toast of your campfire with the mastery of this, the finest of desserts.

SOUND OF MUESLI

Grains! They do a body good! Make your own healthy breakfast, or feed a hungry camp with this fine food.

THAT'S ACCORDION TO YOU

Whether you're playing alone or in a quartet, the accordion song is sweet to any ear. With this badge, Lumberjanes study everything from scales to compositions.

VIEW TO A KILN

Want to know the secret to great pottery? Just add heat!

MARIKO TAMAKI

is a writer known for her graphic novel *This One Summer*, a Caldecott Honor and Printz Honor winner, cocreated with her cousin Jillian Tamaki, among other notable novels. See her work at **marikotamaki.blogspot.com.**

BROOKLYN ALLEN

is a cocreator and the original illustrator of the Lumberjanes graphic novel series and a graduate of the Savannah College of Art and Design. Brooklyn's website is **brooklynaallen.tumblr.com.**

The adventures continue in

BOOK TWO: THE MOON IS UP.

Read on for a sneak peek.

CHAPTER 1

It was early morning at Miss Qiunzella Thiskwin Penniquiqul* Thistle Crumpet's camp for Hardcore Lady-Types, and Jo was lying on her bunk, arms tucked under her head, her brown eyes fixed on the ceiling . . . thinking.

Outside of camp, Jo could spend a whole day lost in thought. Which was a saying Jo didn't like, because it suggested that she was "lost" in thought. And she wasn't lost. She was just . . . thinking.

About what?

Many things, actually.

Including:

The mechanics of pulleys.

Whether she turned her alarm clock off before she left for camp.

* Pronounced *Penny-quee-quellle*

Whether she did or did not see a creature disembark from a moon-like structure a few days ago.

Also, Newton's Law of Motion.

To paraphrase, Newton's Law says that something will keep doing what it's doing, the way it's doing it, until another force shows up and says something like,

Today, this force was April, whose fierce green eyes, framed by her bright, cherry-red hair, peeked over Jo's bunk.

Her booming voice filled the cabin. "Are you ready to begin this, the next chapter in our most adventurous summer?!"

April, one of Jo's best friends since forever and a fellow member of Roanoke cabin, was often described as a force—a force to be reckoned with, a force of nature, and so on.

Today April was in a bit of a hurry because there was a lot to do and . . . Actually, there was always a lot to do. Actually, maybe April was always in a bit of a hurry.

Fortunately, being in a hurry and being a Lumberjane go very well together.

Jo sat up, her head skimming the roof of the cabin as she swung her legs over the side of her bunk. "Yes, I am."

"Indubitably!" April tightened the white bow tied around her hair. "Then let's make like a Lumberjane and get GOING!"

It was another amazingly gorgeous day, and outside the cabin the sky looked like a kid's drawing: deep blue, with three puffy clouds and a bright yellow sun shining down on the summer home away from home of the Lumberjanes.

Was this yet another great day to be a Lumberjane? Yes it was, because, and it's been said before but it is worth repeating, pretty much every day is a great day to be a Lumberjane.

April and Jo charged across the courtyard, past the fire pit and the flagpole, the volleyball nets and the picnic benches, toward the mess hall.

Technically, April was charging, Jo was strolling. Because

April had much shorter legs. Also April liked to CHARGE forward. Jo had very long legs, and she liked to stroll in long, loping strides, hands in pockets. It is a testament to Jo and April's long friendship that they knew how to walk at the exact same speed while walking with completely different paces and strides.

It was probably also a cornerstone of their friendship that April liked to talk as much as Jo liked to be quiet and think.

If Jo and April both liked to talk, it would be a very loud friendship.

April breathed in deeply. "This day is splendidly, vociferously, unquestionably fabulous, is it not? I believe it is."

Jo took a deep breath. It was true. The air smelled like pine, sunshine, and possibility.

Recently, the very adventurous members of Roanoke cabin—April, Jo, Mal, Molly, and Ripley—had charged up a mountain that didn't end up being a mountain but rather a frequently disappearing access route to a society of very laid-back cloud people called Cloudies. This adventure also involved discovering a herd of smelly but magical unicorns.

That was a pretty epic day.

And today was a new day.

And April was ready for more epic-ness.

April rubbed her hands together, her ruby hair glinting

in the sun. "Did you spend your morning of quiet reflection considering how we're going to totally kick butt at Galaxy Wars?"

April said it like a TV game show announcer. *GALAXY WAAARS!*

Jo smiled. Jo's hair was brown and did not glint in the sun, but it was still a very satisfying chestnut color.

"No," she said. "Did you spend your morning of not-so-quiet reflection thinking about how we're going to kick butt at—"

"Why, yes, in fact I did take a moment to reflect on that particular subject during my morning reflections, YES I DID!" April clenched her hands into tiny, powerful fists.

"I mean," she took a preparatory breath. "Of course we're going to rule the camp TO THE MAX at Galaxy Wars. Because we are awesome. And if there WERE a best cabin, which, let's say that most rankings of any sort are subjective, but that you could set a roughly scaled order using a few key components like who is most prepared and most learned, then the most amazing cabin would have to be US!"

Jo paused while April took a deep breath.

Winning was not really as interesting to Jo as many other things. It didn't even make her top-fifty things, if we're honest.

Winning was in April's top-ten interesting things. Currently under April's bunk was a stack of books on stars and planets. Under April's pillow was a dusty encyclopedia volume, *Me–Mo*, which covered subjects including medicine, merchants, monasteries, and, crucially, moons.

"I mean," April said, standing up straight again, "obviously, it's not about winning or losing, that's not what being a Lumberjane is about, and thus it's not what we're about, as Lumberjanes. Obviously it's about having fun, and we will have fun because that's what we do."

And then, April had a crystal-clear thought, and that thought was, *That, and WINNING.*

"Obviously," Jo agreed.

Admittedly, Jo was half listening to April and half thinking about the moon-like craft she thought she saw landing in the trees the other night from her window in the cabin. Jo had followed what for Jo was standard procedure after this sighting, which was to try and collect more information. Which meant jumping out of bed in the middle of the night with her flashlight and rooting through the bushes for an hour, discovering nothing but a wayward nest of squirrels who did not enjoy the intrusion.

Jo wondered if maybe it was a dream.

A very vivid, very awake-feeling dream.

This thought must have registered on Jo's face like a

flicker of light. Like a dragonfly skipping across the calm waters of a summer lake.

April squinted, noticing the flicker. "Hey," she said, and she was about to ask what WAS on Jo's mind, but then the mess hall door swung open, and they were swallowed up by the cacophony of breakfast.

CHAPTER 2

It is important to be VERY, VERY LOUD in the mess hall when you are a Lumberjane. It helps with digestion. If you cannot chew loudly and/or burp loudly, you can also slam your cutlery against the table and/or sing a song, of which, if you are a Lumberjane, there are many. Like that song about the GOAT, the GIRL, and the GARGOYLE playing GOLF. A song that is curiously titled, "Miss Maggy Marple May's Monday."

At the table, Ripley, the smallest but mightiest member of Roanoke cabin, was not singing but defending her pancake record of 14¾. A day earlier, Sally Smithereen of Roswell cabin (who had the record for most milkshakes slurped, at six) came very close to breaking it, except Sally made the rookie mistake of adding a bite of veggie bacon to the mix, and it all went south from there.

As it will.

The key to any record, as any Lumberjane knows, is focus. Which Ripley had, when it came to eating pancakes. When she wasn't eating pancakes, Ripley had a tendency to get distracted by sparkly things. Sparkly was one of Ripley's top-five favorite adjectives, along with fuzzy, bouncy, shiny, and googley.

In addition to eating breakfast, Mal and Molly, two particularly inseparable Roanoke cabin members, were practicing on their accordions for their upcoming That's Accordion to You badges. Successfully completing a badge for music meant performing for Drucilla Johnstone II, the ornery but lovable camp music director and master of multiple instruments, including the tuba, flute, drums, guitar, sitar, recorder, kazoo, harmonica, and violin. Drucilla avoided sunlight at all costs and thought disco was uniformly abominable, but she was a good teacher.

To receive badges, scouts had to play, for Drucilla, without mistakes, a song of their choosing, and three scales.

Music was definitely in Mal's list of favorite things, in addition to problem-solving and being really into Molly. Mal's mother and grandmother had been teaching her to play various instruments since she was old enough to breathe. One of her first stuffed animals was a fluffy drum named BANG.

Running her fingers over the buttons and keys of her accordion, Mal watched Molly, who was looking at her sheet music with great Molly-like intensity.

Before camp, music was not even in Molly's list of favorite one hundred things, although she enjoyed listening to the radio. Before camp, Molly had never even tried to play a musical instrument, but she was kind of digging playing music with Mal, mostly because just about anything she and Mal did together ended up being way more fun than anything Molly did with anyone else. Molly liked it so much she was even thinking of joining Flute Club.

Flute Club, unfortunately, was difficult to join, because they were a very secretive club. And no one really talks about how or where you're supposed to go to join.

Weird.

With Bubbles the raccoon, faithful pet and head warmer, snoozing comfortably on her noggin, Molly squinted at the notes on the page and tried to make her fingers go where they were supposed to go.

"What are you playing for your test tomorrow?" April asked. "Are you playing the classic Lumberjane ditty, 'Miss Tawny Tooberang Tustle's Tuesday'?"

"Is that the one about the hedgehog named Henry who hates horseradish?" Jo asked.

Molly shook her head. "I couldn't find any sheet music for that, so I'm playing 'Frère Jacques' instead." Molly braced her fingers on the keys of her accordion. "It's about a monk who slept in."

"I'm playing Queen's 'Bohemian Rhapsody,' " Mal said, "which is about relationships."

"Holy Siouxsie Sioux." April flopped down on the bench with a plate full of cheese omelette and toast. "Isn't that a really hard song?"

Mal shrugged. "Yeah, I mean, it's a suite containing a multitude of sections that is considered the ultimate hard-rock classical slash prog-rock crossover. No bigs."

"Dude," April nodded appreciatively. "Now that is an operatic undertaking!"

"It's gonna be athom," Ripley said, grinning with a mouth full of pancake.

Jo raised an eyebrow at Ripley. "Hey, Rip. How many pancakes is that?"

Ripley held up all ten sticky fingers.

People have a habit of saying odd and interesting things, like, "Your eyes were bigger than your stomach," which means you thought something was going to be smaller than it was, namely, that you thought a meal or a muffin or a buffet was going to be able to fit into your stomach, but it wasn't. Really, this is a way of saying that your stomach is smaller than you think, because no matter what you eat, your eyes stay pretty much the same size. Maybe it's not worth thinking about. Or maybe it's the key to everything.

Jo had spent a considerable amount of time wondering about whether or not Ripley had an extremely large stomach, or whether she was burning fuel at such a rapid Ripley rate while doing Ripley things that she just needed more fuel.

"Hey," Molly looked up. "Where's Jen?"

"Working on Galaxy Wars, of course," April said.

Galaxy Wars was Roanoke counselor extraordinaire Jen's pet project, if by "pet" we mean "obsession."

"Is it just me or has it been days since we saw her?" Mal wondered out loud. "She hasn't even bothered to leave us a list of chores in, like, three days. Or to tell us to be careful. I don't even know where my socks are anymore."

CLANG! CLANG! CLANG!

"LUMBERJANES! LISTEN UP!"

Camp Director Rosie, Jen, and the rest of the camp counselors stood at the front of the mess hall. Rosie, holding up a massive cast-iron pan and wooden spoon, was doing the clanging.

"LISTEN UP!" Rosie hollered, her voice piercing and loud like freshly sharpened steel.

The din subsided to a low murmur of chewing and curiosity.

Rosie lowered the pan and adjusted her thick cat-eye glasses. "RIGHT! Tonight will kick off our First Annual Lumberjane Galaxy Wars, organized by your very own camp counselors, including Roanoke's very own Jacqueline! Let's give her a hand!"

A roar of volcanic proportions erupted in the hall as all the scouts stood up to applaud their hardworking counselors.

"It's Jen," Jen whispered, clapping while keeping her trusty clipboard tucked under her arm. "Always Jen."

"YEAH, JEN!" Mal cheered.

"WOOT! WOOT!" Ripley yelled.

Jo just smiled, because Jo was less of a "WOOT"-er than her cabin mates.

Jen stepped forward, her counselor uniform crisp, smiling the rosy smile of a nerd about to see her dream take shape.

Jen had many dreams, including a recurring nightmare where she searched for her campers through a complex maze of thick ivy, all while dressed in a set of fuzzy footie pajamas and a baseball hat that said "HONK FOR JUSTICE."

This wasn't one of those dreams.

This was one of those dreams where you work really hard to make something happen, and then it does.

"All right, campers! We're all super excited to bring you this incredible event full of amazing . . . EVENTS!" Jen's eyes sparkled as she gazed out upon the crowd of campers about to take part in this amazing thing. This really amazing thing!

"Ahem," fellow counselor Vanessa nudged Jen, who in gazing had forgotten to mention . . . the events.

"Right!" Jen looked back down at her clipboard. "SO! Galaxy Wars will consist of four days of activities, all taking place after sunset. The first night, tonight, will be a campwide scavenger hunt. Tomorrow night we will have a mystery contest."

April's eyebrows shot up as high as a person's eyebrows could possibly shoot up.

Ripley sighed. "I hope it's a dance off. Bubbles and I have been practicing our cha-cha all week."

Bubbles, who was mostly Molly's pet but also Ripley's dance partner, chirped in the affirmative.

"The next day," Jen continued, "there will be a trivia contest with a distinctly Lumberjane twist!"

Mal hoped it wasn't anything to do with a lake. Or a river. Or water.

"And finally, the pièce de résistance, an all-out obstacle course!"

The mess hall erupted in a raucous cheer.

Lumberjanes love obstacles.

Because obstacles do not stand in the way of being an awesome scout.

Obstacles are what MAKE awesome scouts.

"The cabin that wins each event will receive twenty-five points; the second and third place cabins receive fifteen and ten points. The cabin with the most points at the end of four nights wins! The prize," Jen grinned, "will be announced at the first event tonight."

Jen held up a finger. "Get ready. These events are all night events, so bring your flashlights!"

"Okay, scouts," Vanessa hollered, "you've got the rest of your day to get to your tasks and responsibilities and badges. Zodiac, you have stable duty!"

With yips and yelps of glee, the scouts flooded out of the mess hall.